HIS FATHER'S SON

Autumn Macarthur

ABOUT THE AUTHOR

Autumn Macarthur is a USA Today bestselling author of clean Christian inspirational romances with a strong touch of faith. If you love happy-ever-afters, sweet romance, and Hallmark movies, chances are you'll enjoy her stories!

Originally from Sydney, Australia, she now lives in a small town not far from London, England, with her very English husband (aka The Cat Magnet), and way too many rescue cats for our tiny house! A recent addition to the family are two baby guinea pigs. For such small creatures, they have amazingly huge personalities
.

When she's not feeding cats, she hand sews, reads, and most of all writes heartwarming stories of love and faith. With every story, God teaches her the exact same lessons her hero and heroine need to learn to commit to their forever love.

She's also blessed with a chronic health issue that has changed her life in the way it limits her. It hasn't been easy, but she's come to give thanks for the gift hidden in the illness — the way it's taught her patience, brought her into a greater dependence on God, and given her a far deeper appreciation of His love and provision.

You can visit her at her website http://faithhopeandheartwarming.com, on Facebook as Autumn Macarthur, and on Twitter as @autumnmacarthur. She'd love to hear from you!

Faith, hope, & heartwarming —
inspirational romance to make you smile.

His Fathers Son

Sweetapple Falls #1

See what great love the Father has
lavished on us, that we should be
called children of God!
And that is what we are!
1 John 3:1 NIV

AUTUMN MACARTHUR

Copyright 2017 © by Autumn Macarthur

First Print Edition, June 2017

ISBN-13: 9781521716625

Published by Faith, Hope, & Heartwarming
http://faithhopeandheartwarming.com

BIBLE VERSION COPYRIGHT NOTICES

DEDICATION

Love to my dear husband Arthur for our adventure of marriage, where I'm growing in love and learning what commitment means, even in the toughest times.

Thanks to Shannon, crit partner and dear friend, whose insight into relationships is so deep and so true. I value your support so much!

Thanks most of all to God, for making us His loved adopted children, for always loving us, always forgiving us, and always being willing to give us second chances, when we ask Him.

And thank you, dear reader, for reading. I do hope you enjoy the story and are blessed by it.

CHAPTER ONE

ANNA HARRISON ENDED THE CALL, replacing the old beige handset into its wall-mounted cradle with a sigh of relief. Thankfully, her oven timer's ding cut short Maggie's latest matchmaking attempt. Why couldn't her sweet older friend refuse to believe she could be happy being a single mom?

Well, she was.

Few men would accept the amount of care her son Josh needed, or love him the way she did. After twelve years of just the two of them, the idea of adding a third person to their family wasn't even on the table.

They managed fine. Josh could grow up in the same home she had. Her paintings of Sweetapple Falls sold well during in the tourist season, earning enough to get by.

And they had cookies.

She opened the oven door, inhaling the sweet aroma of chocolate chips and walnuts. Josh's favorite, and hers too. Tugging on threadbare oven mitts, she lifted out the cookie tray and smiled at her kitchen like it was an old friend.

Sure, the sunshine yellow walls needed repainting. The stove was the same avocado green one Mom had cooked on. The cracked linoleum caught at her bare feet in the summer. No matter.

This stuff had been around long enough to become vintage and almost Pinterest-worthy. The old house might need repairs, but it didn't need a man to make it home.

Josh's wheelchair motor whirred behind her and a skinny arm snaked past to nab a cookie. He ate non-stop, but stayed way too thin. Her heart twisted, as it always did at the sight of him.

Every minute with Josh was a gift to treasure.

"Joshua Harrison, leave the cookies alone! They're too hot." Her scolding tone sounded harsh, but he'd see straight through it. She couldn't be hard on him, and he knew it.

He pulled his hand back anyway.

"Are these for tonight? Please?" He put on his best pleading puppy-dog face, with the lopsided grin she adored.

But the intense blueness of his eyes jolted her. As he got older, Josh reminded her more and more of his father. She pushed the thought out of her mind. His father disappeared from their lives long ago. It was just her and Josh, the way it always had been.

Her lips curved at his shameless wheedling. "I thought they'd be a nice way to celebrate a good week. You've made it through winter without a single chest infection. You brought home a straight-A mid-term report. And Maggie told me she sold a big painting for us. We can get the roof repaired at last."

Josh raised victory fists high as he could reach, barely above his shoulders. "Yay!"

She chuckled. "Is that for the roof, or the cookies? Don't get too excited. There's only this one tray. I had to save some chocolate chips to make the dessert."

Seeing the hopeful questions in his eyes, she lifted one hand in a stop sign. "Yes, you can scrape the bowl. No, you can't eat any tonight. It's for tomorrow's fundraiser."

"Okay." He smiled.

No sulkiness, no complaints.

Josh put a cheerful twist on almost everything, including the difficulties he faced. His optimism stilled her own moans, reminding her to count all the small, everyday blessings. She walked around the island counter to give him a quick hug.

"Aw, Mom." His words held the please-don't-embarrass-me tone usually reserved for when his friends were around. Even so, Anna figured a hug from Mom now and then let him know he was loved.

Feeling skin and bones beneath her hands — no muscle — as he leaned into her arms, she wondered yet again how God could do this to her son. As always, the question remained unanswered.

Josh let her hug him, then used his wheelchair controls to scoot back. "Those cookies will be cool enough now, won't they?"

Though she longed to cling, she let him go.

He devoured a warm cookie in two big bites, and she passed him another. One for her, too. A sigh escaped her as the sweet chocolatey hit kicked in. Her mom's recipe worked every time, tasting of comfort and home.

The pet flap in the back door banged and small feet clattered on the floor as a streak of black and white darted across the kitchen to land on Josh's lap. He grunted as sixteen pounds of high-speed piglet smacked into him. "Slow down, Pattie Pork Pie!" His thin fingers stroked his pet's bristled head while she snuffled for crumbs.

"Pattie doesn't know what slow down means." Shaking her head, she laughed. Josh asked for very little, so when he'd seen Pattie at the animal shelter, it had been hard to refuse him. But maybe the pot-bellied piglet was one time she should have said no.

Josh fed Pattie a chunk of his cookie. "There. Greater love has no kid than he gives up his cookie for his pig."

"Porky girl needs something healthier to eat, or she'll grow to the size of a bus." She reached into the refrigerator and pulled out some lettuce leaves for Pattie to chow on. "I'm not sure the Lord will appreciate your paraphrase, either."

He laughed. "God won't mind. He gave me my sense of humor, didn't He?"

Josh had a comeback for everything.

"At least, skip that line in your act tomorrow night at the fundraiser?"

Cookie crumbs edged his grin. "Deal! I'll take Pattie for her afternoon walk now, before the guys arrive."

"Let me help you." She moved around the counter, headed for the coat rack.

He pushed his wheelchair control to top speed and beat her there, beaming in triumph. "I can do it."

No. He couldn't. That was the problem. Something as simple as putting on his jacket could exhaust Josh.

The front doorbell rang, leaving her arguments unspoken.

Everyone in Sweetapple Falls knew to come to the back. The front door meant flowers, strangers, or bad news. Stifling her twinge of apprehension, she laughed. "Saved from the smother mother. I'll get the door."

"What if it's another weirdo who saw us on TV and wants to marry you? Should I call Deputy Connor?"

So sweet that he wanted to protect her. She smiled and touched his cheek. "It's okay, honey. It's been weeks since the last one. I'll keep the chain on the door."

Most likely, it was one of Josh's friends, using the front door for a joke. But the figure she glimpsed through the frosted glass was way too tall for that. Maybe she'd been too quick to tell Josh not to call the Deputy. Heart accelerating, she pushed the chain firmly into place before unlatching the door and peering through the narrow gap.

A man with hair the same rich brown as Josh stood on her porch. Stubble darkened his strong jaw. Hope and hesitation mingled in eyes she remembered so well, the warm cobalt blue of a summer sky, now edged by a network of fine lines.

Shock shuddered through her. Only grasping the door frame kept her upright.

"Anna?"

Her startled stare collided with his, and caught. The moment stretched, impossibly long, something twanging in the air between them. She struggled to remember how to breathe.

"Anna," he repeated, with conviction this time. He smiled, the slow sweet bad-boy grin that made her heart somersault in her chest at eighteen.

Even at thirty, it still did.

Luke Tanner. The last man she expected to see in Sweetapple Falls.

She froze in place, staring up at the man she'd once loved.

The anger that powered Luke through a two-thousand mile journey vanished as soon as he saw Anna. Instead of antagonism, wild joy at her nearness surprised him, pounding in his blood.

He reached a hand toward her without thinking, but she jerked back.

The questioning smile she'd opened the door with vanished as she recognized him, a hand lifting to cover her mouth. "Luke. No. You can't be here." She breathed the barely audible words. Confusion left her green eyes cloudy as uncut emeralds.

His arm dropped to his side. He hadn't expected she'd put out the welcome mat for him, but he'd hoped...

Crazy to hope. Her white-faced stare and the chained door reminded him of all that lay between them. Their son's entire lifetime. A mountain of secrets and lies.

Anna glanced behind her, then undid the chain and stepped onto the porch, pulling the door shut after her. She stationed herself in front of it, an unmistakable "Keep Out" sign separating him from the golden glow of light and the whiff of freshly baked cookies.

Realization sucker punched him. She wanted to stop him seeing someone in the house, or stop someone seeing him.

Josh. Their son. It had to be.

"What are you doing here?" Her soft voice echoed with stunned surprise. Then raising her chin, she pushed her blonde hair back from her face, and her lips tightened. "You can't just turn up on my doorstep with no warning."

Rubbing the bump on his nose, he stood his ground against her flash of resentment. He wouldn't leave till he discovered the truth. "I'm here because I saw you and Josh on that TV talent show."

The sweetness fled from her face, leaving her every inch Deputy Harrison's daughter. She glared at him, narrow-eyed. "Why? Do you feel sorry for him? Or me?" Acid edged her words.

He shook his head and opened his mouth to reply, but she charged right on.

"If that's why you're here, forget it. We had plenty of that when *Talent Trek* first aired. We don't need or want anyone treating us as pity cases. You didn't put up much of a fight to be his father twelve years ago. Why come back now claiming to care?"

Luke stiffened. Of course he'd felt sorry when he saw the brave, funny kid calling himself the "Wheelchair Cowboy" do his comedy act. Then he'd seen Anna, and realized the boy was their son. "I cared. I've always cared." Emotion vibrated through him as his heart clenched with memory. That one time he'd held Josh....

"You couldn't get away fast enough." She almost stamped her foot.

"I wanted to be Josh's father. I wanted to marry you, to make us a family." He blew out a low angry breath. "You refused to marry me and signed adoption papers, instead. *That's* when I left."

Anna ducked her head, and hugged her arms across her chest. "We were both eighteen, Luke. Just kids. We could never have made it work."

"We could have tried." He forced air into stiff lungs and gritted out the words. "And now I find you kept Josh. You cheated me of knowing my son. And cheated Josh out of his father."

Even as he spoke, doubt shook him. Could be, she was right. If she'd married him, would he have dragged her and Josh down with him, too?

"You went away. As soon as you saw I'd signed the papers, you signed on the dotted line too, then left." Her voice held a touch of little-girl-lost.

When she raised her head, for a heart-stopping instant she looked no older than she had at eighteen, despite the faint new lines creasing her eyes.

Compassion swelled in him, and he reached out to her again. She wrapped her arms around herself tighter and retreated against the door. He stepped back. Anna had always had that wariness, like a shy wild bird. The only way to stop her flying away was to keep his distance.

"Your father told me I'd ruined your life, and leaving was the only way to make things right." His jaw tightened, remembering the ugly scene when Sheriff Harrison found him at the hospital with Anna and newborn Josh. "I thought you wanted me to leave."

"Why would you think that?" Bewilderment glazed her eyes.

"Hard not to, when you sided with your dad about giving up Josh. You didn't ask me to stay." The pain of her rejection still burned, as fresh as it had back then.

Biting her lip, she said nothing, and glanced down, avoiding his gaze.

"At least tell me what happened to Josh. I though the doctor who checked him said he was healthy? Was he injured?" He poured all the concern he felt for his son into his voice.

If they focused on Josh, maybe they could stop their pointless bickering.

For a moment she tensed, and he suspected she'd tell him it was none of his business. Then she slumped against the cracked blue paint on the old timber door. Sadness darkened her eyes.

"The doctor got it wrong. A few hours after you left, they rushed Josh to the NICU. At first they didn't know what was wrong. Then at three months, the doctors diagnosed a rare form of muscular dystrophy. It's a life-limiting condition, but they can't say how limiting. He's already lived longer than they told me he would."

Everything in him stilled as her words hit. Anna endured this every day — living with the knowledge their son would get sicker.

He had to stay.

No matter what she said, how she rejected him, he wouldn't walk away this time. He'd be a father to his son, and support Anna as much as she'd let him.

"So now you know, I suppose you'll leave again?" Despite the accusation edging her voice, a hint of vulnerability caught at his heart. Did she regret some of her choices, the same way he did?

Luke dragged in a deep breath, unable to read the expression darkening her hazel eyes. Anna was complicated. She always had been. Way out of his league.

But they'd fallen in love anyway, and had a son.

"I didn't leave willingly." He kept his reply gentle rather than reacting to her words. "I thought you'd realize that."

As if he'd pushed a button, she stiffened and threw back her head, resentment coming off her in waves. "All I know is that you weren't here when we needed you most. I tried to contact you when we knew what was wrong with Josh, and you'd vanished. You're twelve years too late, Luke."

"It's not too late to let me be a father to my son, the way I wanted to be." Despite his good intentions, hot words rose to his mouth. "You told me you'd agreed with your father, chosen to have him adopted. Did getting rid of me mean more to you than your honesty?"

A whisper deep inside asked who he was angry with — Anna or himself?

He'd left, despairing over her rejection, and raced straight into the stupidest mistakes he could make. Guilt twisted his gut. She'd lied to him, but he had far more to regret.

"I never lied." She took a step toward him, fists balled, chin raised with a stubbornness he didn't remember.

He stared at her, without speaking. If she'd shown some of this spirit and stood up to her father's demands twelve years ago, if she'd given him a chance instead of obeying the Deputy, things could have turned out so differently.

"I did agree to the adoption, though it broke my heart. And so did you." Her hands lifted, covering her eyes as if even the memory hurt. "Then the doctors said he might die. I couldn't leave him alone in the hospital, risk him being abandoned with no love. Dad relented and let me bring him home. And where were you then? Long gone." Her lip curled.

He stared at the weather-worn timber boards beneath his feet. Forcing out a long hard breath, he deliberately loosened his tense muscles and unclenched his rigid jaw.

Lord, give me the words.

Straightening, he met her glare. "I'm sorry. I shouldn't have accused you of dishonesty. We both had tough decisions to make."

She nodded, her tight expression softening. "We did. So where did you go?"

"Eugene, for a couple of months. Back with my old foster parents." He swallowed. Anna mustn't know too much about that time, but he wouldn't lie to her, either. "Then I needed to get right away. I joined a house-building charity, and I've been working in Latin America ever since."

Her lips twisted in an attempt at a smile. "Okay. That explains the tan in March. Not from taking it easy on a beach somewhere." She reached out in a butterfly touch, her hand pale against his darker skin.

The brief contact sent a surge of warmth along his arm, snatching his breath. Then she flinched and pulled back. Apprehension sparked her eyes as she wrapped her arms defensively across her chest. So she'd felt it too, their instinctive response to each other. A complication neither of them needed.

He'd come to Sweetapple Falls to be Josh's father, nothing more.

CHAPTER TWO

LUKE BACKED OFF FAST. He had no intention of attempting to reignite the love they'd once shared. Anna's equally quick retreat suggested she'd welcome it about as much as a rattlesnake on her porch.

Focus on her question, not his unwanted reaction to her.

"Far from taking it easy," he replied. "We worked with the poorest people in rural villages and city slums, providing them with materials and skills to build their own homes. I had no plans to come back. I hadn't set foot in the U.S. again till today. But then I saw you and Josh on the village's one TV."

Anna rolled her eyes. "You always were impulsive. Phoning or emailing first didn't occur to you?"

"Your college email bounced. Mail from Mexico is slow. You've changed your cellphone number, I'm guessing, because when I tried the old one, I got someone else. And I figured someone would hang up on me if I called your number here."

"Probably." Her lips twisted wryly.

He shrugged and smiled. "So when the charity's CEO gave me leave to take the next flight out, it seemed best to fly straight here than try to reach you any other way."

A whirring on the other side of the door stopped her replying. She raised a finger to her lips and threw him a warning glance.

"Mom, are you okay? Do you need me to make that call?"

Josh. His son, only a few inches away.

"I'm fine. It's just someone I used to know a long time ago. From way back when I was in college."

Someone she used to know. The casual dismissal wrenched Luke. Though it was true.

Apart from the undeniable fact they'd created a child together.

"Can I take Pattie for a walk now?" Josh asked. His dog, or a younger sister?

"Wait till I'm back indoors. He'll be leaving any minute." The sharp glance she threw Luke told him she'd make sure of it.

"Okay, Mom." The whirring started again and then faded.

An old wound ripped open as Josh moved away, the grief carved deep into Luke's heart that day in the hospital when Anna told him she was giving up their son. "When can I meet him?"

Anna turned to him, hands raised like stop signs in front of her chest. "I didn't expect this." Her hands dropped to her side, and hurt shadowed her eyes. "If you'd come back sooner, I doubt I would even have spoken to you. It's taken a long time for my anger at how easy you gave up to fade. You can't meet him yet."

"So you *will* let me see our son?" Hope flared, sudden and bright.

"Not yet," she repeated. "I need to know you won't leave when the going gets tough. Being a father isn't something you can pick up when you feel like it, especially with a kid like Josh."

The doubtful, untrusting edge to her voice sliced him. Truth was, he had no idea if he could do this. What did he know about being a father? His mom couldn't even tell him who his own dad was.

I can do all things through Christ…

He couldn't do it. But God could.

Rubbing the bridge of his nose, he silently prayed for help. "I wanted our baby to grow up with a mother who love him, in a settled home. And with a father." Everything he hadn't had himself. "You've given him two out of three. The third is my job. I'll find a way to be here for Josh."

She shook her head. "He needs stability in his life. I won't risk letting him get close to you."

Tension knotted him. She wasn't giving an inch. The Anna he'd known had been soft and sweet and forgiving, with no trace of this hard-edged resolve.

Then something so obvious he should have thought of it sooner hit like a punch in the gut. "Anna, is there's another reason you don't want me around? Is there a man in your life?"

His breath hitched as he waited for her reply.

"No, there's no one else." She exhaled hard, as if annoyed by his question. "Being a single mom doesn't leave a lot of time for dating. Being single mom to a disabled kid, even less." Burdens heavier than she should have to bear weighted her voice and sagged her shoulders. "That's not the issue here."

Relief rocked him, out of proportion to anything he had the right to feel. This wasn't about him and Anna, it was about Josh. "You have your parents' support, but it's not the same as having your child's father to help. You must wish at times you had someone else to share the load. Let me be that person."

A short, almost bitter laugh escaped her. "I have no support. And I've managed just fine. Mom and Dad both died in an accident, before Josh turned three. They left me, just like you did." She rubbed her hands over her face. "Give me time, Luke. I need more time. You can't expect to simply walk into Josh's life, or mine."

If he wanted to be involved with his son, he didn't have much choice but to wait. "I know this is hard for you. We have a lot to discuss and a lot to decide. I'm not going anywhere."

"I hope not, Luke. For Josh's sake." A sigh escaped her and her grief-shadowed eyes met his. "You can't imagine how I felt when you walked out that hospital door, leaving me."

He glimpsed the old Anna. Soft, open, unguarded. The same grief echoed in his heart.

"I'm sorry. We made a mess of things. Both of us." He handed her the note he'd planned to leave in the mailbox if no one answered the door. "I'm staying at the Sweetapple Lodge. Here's my cellphone number."

As she leaned closer to take it, he caught a subtle hint of the same scented shampoo he remembered smelling in her hair. The scent transported him back twelve years, to when they'd been young, hopeful, and crazy in love.

Memories he needed to forget.

"Josh and I have a busy day tomorrow, but I'll call you when I can. I need to go now." She nodded goodbye, then slipped back into the house, shutting the door behind her. Not with a slam. With a quiet final click, closing him out of her life, and Josh's.

A reminder how little he meant to her now.

When he'd seen Josh on TV, it seemed God had given him a second chance to be the father he'd wanted to be. But he'd need to work harder to convince Anna to give him a second chance.

Much harder.

Anna slumped against the door, breath trapped in her throat as she waited for Luke's footsteps to retreat across the porch decking.

At last, he was gone.

Her hands formed fists, pressing against her closed eyes. She would not cry. She would not.

The flood of emotions dammed up for all these years, threatening to crash through her carefully constructed defenses, wouldn't overwhelm her. Time to hold on to Mom's advice.

You can get through anything by simply doing whatever comes next. One step at a time.

What came next was pretending nothing had happened. Making sure Josh enjoyed his usual Friday pizza and movie night with his friends. Later, once he was in bed, she could think about what to do.

Straightening, she pinned on a smile worthy of the mom in a Toll House cookie ad and went to find Josh. Giving him the best life she could, that was what mattered.

Not Luke. And certainly not her feelings.

Somehow, she made it through the boys' movie night. She smiled and laughed while serving pizza and sodas and cookies. She prepared the dessert for tomorrow night's fundraiser. She washed up. She worked out a new budget for the month. They could afford the roof repairs, just.

The whole time, she unobtrusively kept watch over Josh and the guys. They were good kids, but Josh tired easily and didn't always recognize his limits. Plus, keeping busy gave her no chance to examine her reactions to Luke's return.

Too soon though, the other boys left, collected by their parents, and Josh lay drowsy on his bed.

"There you go, torture session over." As she snuggled his comforter over him, she used his nickname for their physical therapy sessions. Only half-joking. The stretches necessary to prevent muscle contractures inevitably hurt him.

And he had to endure them twice a day.

Josh gave an exaggerated sigh of relief and then stared up at her. His wide eyes, so like his father's, held a question. Bracing herself for what he might ask, she took a deep breath. As Josh neared his teens, the questions he asked made "Why is the sky blue?" seem easy.

"Alex's father said he'd take him skiing if he got just one A. Noah's and George's dads did, too. I got A's. So can we go with them?"

Her heart sank as Josh continued, sleepy but enthusiastic.

"I looked it up on the Internet. There's snow right into April. They have special equipment for kids like me and they do lessons, too." He made a show of holding his breath, and crossed his fingers awkwardly. "I really want to. Please?"

A sense of failure bit her. She wanted so much to give him everything. But she'd had to quit her job when he'd last been in hospital, and her paintings barely provided enough to get by.

"I'm sorry, Josh. If I could scrape up the money for a trip I would, but we can't rely on buckets in the attic any longer. Getting our leaky roof reshingled will clean us out financially."

His face fell, but only for a second. "Next winter, right?"

"Right." She smiled, though she ached for him. They both knew his illness meant they couldn't plan too far ahead.

His brow creased. "There's something else I want to ask. I've been wondering all evening. That man who was here earlier, did he know my dad?"

Panic clutched her chest. She'd never lie to Josh, but she wasn't ready to tell him the truth yet, either. "What makes you think that?"

"You said it was someone from college. You met my dad while you were away at college. I just thought..." Yearning and longing twisted his thin face.

She closed her eyes for a moment, struggling for the right words to ease his hurt and loss. "Josh, I know you want your dad. But you have plenty of other men in your life. Pastor Dan. Deputy Connor. Your teachers. Your friends' dads. All good, honest, reliable men."

She didn't add — *not like your father.* Truthfulness made her admit resentment fueled the uncharitable thought. After so many years, she didn't know Luke.

Josh's mouth puckered. "Yeah. But they're not the same as having my own dad."

She reached out a hand to smooth the floppy brown hair back from his forehead. "I'm sorry."

Was she doing right not telling him? Doubt tightened her stomach. Surely it was best to wait till she could trust Luke wouldn't leave again. How could she risk Josh growing to love and depend on Luke, only to have him go?

Forcing a chuckle, she attempted a joke. "You find me a man you want as your dad, and I'll marry him."

"Mom." Josh stretched the word out to a whole sentence worth of exasperation.

Pretending to pout, she fluffed her hair. "You don't think he'd have me?"

Josh giggled drowsily then drifted into sleep. Anna stayed beside his bed, gazing down at him. Then she flicked off the light, leaving the night light in the corner glowing, the same as every night since she'd brought him home as a baby. She left the door ajar as she always did, so she'd hear from her room if he needed her.

Tonight, her bedroom didn't feel the cozy comfortable haven it usually did. Josh's question challenged her with the need to decide what to do about Luke.

She rubbed her hands over her face, and opened the closet door. On the top shelf, right at the back, a flat brown cardboard box lay hidden, unopened since she brought Josh home from the hospital. Reaching on tiptoe, she pulled it out and placed it on her bed. She wasn't sure why she'd kept it, but she had.

Lifting the lid unleashed all the feelings she'd shut away. She stared at the contents. A couple of cards Luke gave her while they were dating, and a single photo. Emotion wrenched her, a deep tearing pain.

The cards, she'd ignore. The few words clumsily lettered in them meant nothing to her now, though they'd seemed to promise so much at seventeen. Living away from home for the first time, thrilled to be accepted to a fine arts pre-degree course in Eugene, she'd been idealistic, naive, and ripe to fall in love.

Too young to be away from home.

When she'd gotten lost in a bad part of town after an evening gallery visit and Luke turned up to protect her from a threatening gang, he seemed the hero she'd dreamed of. By the time she clung behind him as he returned her to her college dorm on his old motorbike, she imagined she'd met the boy she'd make a family with and grow old alongside.

No matter that he was barely literate and worked as a laborer. Their love would conquer all.

Then, after six months of dating, she discovered the one time they'd gone too far had consequences.

He'd made so many promises. Promised to marry her as soon as she turned eighteen and didn't need her dad's permission. Promised to take care of her and the baby, to work hard and find them an apartment. Promised he'd love her always.

Turned out Luke's "always" hadn't lasted long.

How could she trust him now?

Putting the cards to one side, she picked up the photo tucked beneath them and held it in trembling fingers.

A younger Anna sat in a hospital bed, tired but proud. Wrapped in a white blanket and just an hour old, tiny Josh snuggled in her arms. Luke stood beside them, bending to touch the baby's cheek with a gentle finger.

His look of tender and astonished wonder twisted her heart. He truly *had* wanted to be a father. Seeing the raw emotion shining on Luke's face, it couldn't be denied.

Then Dad arrived and started a huge angry confrontation, demanding Luke leave her alone.

He'd insisted they were too young. That Luke wasn't good enough for her, and the baby would have a better life if she let him be adopted. Terrified things might end in a fight that would land Luke in jail, she'd backed down. Given in to Dad's orders.

She'd never been able to stand up to him. No one could. Deputy Sheriff Harrison's word was law.

And he was right about them being too young. Fiercely in love with her newborn, she wanted the best for him. She wasn't sure she and Luke could give him that. Love wasn't always enough.

Maybe she'd been wrong. Maybe if Luke had stayed around, if he'd been stronger too, she could have stood up to Dad. Maybe they could have made it work. But Luke stormed out of the hospital and didn't come back. Didn't answer her calls. Didn't return her texts. She'd never heard from him again until today.

His return changed everything.

At least she didn't need to fear anyone would recognize Luke and tell Josh the truth. The nearest he'd been to Sweetapple Falls was the hospital in Orchard Bridge where Josh was born.

Mom and Dad were the only people here who'd met him, and they were gone.

Grief hit her like a blow to the chest, and she hugged her arms around herself. Josh had no other family. Only her. She couldn't refuse him the chance to know his father.

If Luke stayed, she'd permit him to be part of Josh's life.

But he'd need to prove himself. He'd have to convince her he meant to stay around. She was sure of just one thing. When Luke left before, he'd broken her heart.

She wouldn't allow him to do the same to their son.

CHAPTER THREE

LUKE PLACED HIS ORDER at the counter of Sweetapple Falls' one diner, then looked for somewhere to sit. Half the town's population must be in Maggie's on Main for Saturday brunch.

He took the little rickety table near the door, leaving the four-seater at the window for a family, and looked around while he waited. Homey, country-style décor created a welcoming air.

Paintings lined the walls. A huge blue and green one hinted at a landscape, drawing him in, giving a sense of peace. After seeing Anna yesterday, he surely needed peace. Hours spent praying left him no nearer a solution.

All he knew was that he had to stay. How and where, he had no idea.

He had to place that in God's hands, and trust.

From here he couldn't make out the price on the little white card under the painting, but he guessed it wouldn't be cheap. If he had more spare cash, he'd buy the painting. Show Anna he really was staying, putting down roots here. But he didn't want to spend more than he had to until he knew how easy it would be to find work.

Besides, impulsively purchasing art because it appealed to him, when he didn't have a wall to hang it on, probably wasn't the best way to prove he was good father material.

The older woman with startling orange hair who'd taken his order placed a steaming coffee and a sizable serving of apple pie on his table. He breathed deep, savoring the aroma.

The waitress's name badge showed Maggie herself served him. She wiped her hands on the bright floral pink apron wrapped around her ample waist.

"I saw you admiring the artwork. It's by Anna Harrison, a well-known local artist. A lovely girl. How she finds time to paint I don't know, looking after a sick son on her own."

Anna.

Anna did these amazing paintings.

Shock stuttered his heartbeat. When they met, she'd been studying fine arts, but shied away from showing him her work. He'd guessed she was talented, or she wouldn't be in that course. But he hadn't realized *how* talented. Even with his non-existent knowledge of art, surely these paintings were fit to grace any gallery in the country.

Would this chatty woman be so friendly if she knew he was the absent father of Anna's disabled son, the reason she'd had to give up her art course?

Fighting down a wave of guilt, he forced a smile for Maggie. "Her work is very good. But right now, I'm more interested in what you brought me. It's been a while since I ate."

"Enjoy. Refill your coffee from the carafe whenever you want. No need to ask. And if you decide on buying a painting, just let me know. I'll be happy to help you." She beamed and bustled off.

He took a forkful of the pie. The sweet crumbly pastry and tart filling were perfection. But the reminder of all he'd taken from Anna meant he might as well eat sawdust.

Lord, why? I had everything all mapped out. And now this.

Three days ago, sitting in that cantina celebrating wrapping up a successful project with his crew, things seemed so sure and certain. His boss had insisted he take a couple of weeks from the months of leave he'd accumulated, rather than move straight on to the next job. He'd planned to revisit a few past projects, catch up with the local guys, and lend a hand with whatever they had going on.

Then a chance glimpse of kid in a wheelchair on a TV talent show sent him charging back to Oregon and an uncertain future.

But how could he not come back, when he'd seen Anna with the boy in the after-act interviews and realized who the kid was? Josh's jokes about not having a father made it clear the boy longed for a dad.

So his instant response — rush to tell his son, "I'm here."

He couldn't blame Anna for wanting to protect Josh. He could only hope that once she trusted him, her attitude would change. That she'd give him the chance to be the father he'd always intended to be.

When he'd gone to the hospital after Josh's birth, he'd hoped she'd change her mind, agree to marry him. He'd worked so hard, to show her he could provide for a family. Angry and hurting that she thought he wasn't good enough to be a husband and father, he'd left.

She'd made her choice, and it wasn't him.

He had no way of knowing she'd see that as him abandoning her. And he'd had no way of knowing Josh would get sick and the adoption Anna agreed to wouldn't happen.

No wonder she'd been so upset when he turned up last night accusing her of lying to get rid of him.

He squeezed his eyes shut. Things must have been tough for her. Even tougher after her parents died. Orphaned at twenty-one, alone in that big house with a sick child…

No doubt she'd done a great job as a single mom, unlike his own messed-up mother, but his son shouldn't have to go any longer without a father.

First step — prove to her he truly was staying.

He walked to the newspaper rack and chose a copy of the local paper to leaf through as he ate breakfast. Looked as if Sweetapple Falls was a good, safe place, somewhere people had community spirit.

Either that, or the newspaper employed Pollyanna as the editor.

No wonder Anna had been so innocent and trusting when they'd met. How different would his life have been if he'd grown up in a town like this? He could imagine settling here. Something about Sweetapple Falls said home. The timber and mellow red-brick buildings, reeking of gold-rush era history. The wide, tree-lined streets. The way it nestled into the surrounding hills. The friendliness and welcome of the townsfolk.

All but one, that is.

Anna would get used to the idea. He was staying.

Finding the employment page in the paper, he smiled. Building jobs within driving distance. Not that he needed to look for paying work yet. When he called the office to speak to his boss last night, Larry insisted he remain on paid leave, as he hadn't taken more than a few days' vacation the whole time he'd worked for them. An article in the newspaper said the town's church needed volunteers for a building project.

Perfect. While he helped with that, he could look around for other work, buy a cheap truck, and get everything else he'd need sorted out. Like finding somewhere to stay. He flicked to the rentals section.

The old fashioned bell over the entrance door jangled, and he looked up from the newspaper. Anna struggled to push the door open with her back while maneuvering a large flat object way too big for her outstretched arms. Probably another painting.

He jumped to open the door for her.

"Thanks," she said, without glancing at him.

"Let me help." Luke took hold of her awkward load.

She turned then, eyes startled, and pulled her burden back, shaking her head.

Luke let go. He wouldn't risk damaging it. Plus, the interested stares of the other diners burned into his back. Friendly as the town seemed, Maggie already proved how easily small-town tongues wagged.

Josh's father suddenly appearing would cause gossip enough. He and Anna would have to discuss how to handle that. No need to cause more.

"I can manage. If you move out of my way, I'll get the painting where it needs to go." Her tone was carefully bland, but her eyes flashed a challenge.

Why was she so stubborn about taking help?

Or was it just help from him?

A man wearing a brown sheriff's uniform came to the door behind her. Luke tensed, his instincts on alert. Despite the many years since he'd lived on the streets, he hadn't lost the reflex response.

Lawmen meant danger.

The deputy looked from Anna to Luke and the easy smile he'd walked in with turned tight and suspicious.

"This man bothering you?" he asked Anna, with more than a hint of warning for Luke. He placed his hand on her lower back with a proprietary air.

Hairs rose on the nape of Luke's neck.

She twisted to smile up at the deputy. Those sunshine smiles of hers used to warm Luke all the way through. Now, she gave them to another man. Jealousy he had no right to feel knifed through him.

"It's okay, Connor," Anna said. "He offered to help. I was just explaining I *can* manage fine on my own." She moved a little, away from his possessive touch. "And before you offer as well, I can manage on my own."

The deputy let his hand drop.

Luke's shoulders lost some of their hard tension. He forced his hands to loosen as he moved out of Anna's way.

She hauled the painting to the counter, giving that same warm smile to Maggie.

So he was the only one to get the Siberian treatment. Okay. He could live with that. It would take her a while to get used to the idea of him being around.

Connor filled his coffee mug from the carafe, raised it with a "Thank you," to Maggie, and headed for the door.

"See you tonight. Seven o'clock, right?" Anna called after him.

The deputy looked back from the door and grinned. "I'll be there. Wouldn't miss it." On his way out, he gave Luke a warning glare that said loud as if he'd spoken, *Keep away from my girl.* The bell jangled as the door closed behind him.

Luke glanced at Anna, back turned to him, blonde braid bouncing on her shoulder as she resumed her animated chat to Maggie.

Clearly, she had him on ignore.

Clearly, she could manage just fine without him.

And could Josh, too?

He slumped at the table, staring at the newspaper with sightless eyes. He'd raced up here wanting to be a father to his son. But wouldn't the deputy, a home town hero like Anna's dad, make a far better father than he ever could?

What a no-brainer.

He threw enough cash on the table to cover his order plus a generous tip, then walked out the door. The bell ringing over his head sounded a death knell to his hope of setting right his past mistakes.

Could be, the best thing to do for Anna and Josh was to walk right out of their lives again.

Anna watched Luke leave the diner and stalk off down the street, in the opposite direction from Connor.

That scene between them unnerved her. If the two men were dogs, they'd have circled each other with hackles raised. She'd just about heard them growl.

Ridiculous. She wasn't some juicy bone they could fight over.

After his wife Suzy's death, for more than a few years now, she'd known Connor hoped she'd date him. Her gentle hints that wouldn't ever happen, but she'd gladly be his friend, had clearly been too gentle.

How could she be more than friends with any man, when she hadn't forgotten the only man she'd ever loved?

As for Luke, he couldn't expect to appear and pick up like the last twelve years never happened. Sure, he'd been angry and upset when she'd caved to Dad. Sure, she couldn't ignore the unwanted jolt her heart had given, seeing him here in the diner.

She cared for Josh too much to let him get involved with a deadbeat dad.

Luke needed to prove himself before she'd let him anywhere near their son. And near her — forget it.

"You two know each other?" Maggie asked. "He admired your paintings. Stared at that one closest to the door for the longest time."

Anna dragged her gaze away from Luke's retreating back. She'd have to be careful. Maggie's bright eyes didn't miss a thing. "Did he?" She did her best to sound like she didn't care one bit.

How much dared she say? Maggie was the kindest person in Sweetapple Falls, and the biggest gossip too. Her diner wasn't known as the real Town Crier office for nothing. Chuck Lucas, the editor, gathered much of the local news from his usual corner table.

Anna gave Chuck a wave and an overly perky smile before she answered Maggie, choosing her words carefully. "I met him in Eugene, back when I was in college. He must just be passing through town."

She hoped her voice held the casual note she aimed for. She'd made sure not to lie. Not telling the whole truth wasn't the same as telling a lie, was it? Maybe she should cross her fingers and ask God for forgiveness just in case.

"Fine looking man," Maggie said. "For someone passing through, he seemed mighty interested in the job vacancies and property rentals pages in the Crier." She peered at Anna, hopeful as a meadowlark eyeing a juicy bug.

Anna's hands tightened on the picture frame. Dared she hope, too?

For Josh's sake, of course, not her own. Luke Tanner staying in town meant nothing to her personally. Her only concern was for Josh. The boy wanted his father so badly.

Avoiding Maggie's too-observant gaze, she regarded her fingers as if they belonged to someone else. They'd pressed onto the timber hard enough to make her nails white. Deliberately, she relaxed them.

"Was he?" she repeated, doing her best to sound uninterested.

People didn't change. Not that much. He'd left before, when in her secret heart she'd longed for him to help her stand up to Dad. She couldn't let herself hope or trust that Luke would settle here.

Life hadn't been perfect, but it *had* been tranquil. Luke's arrival changed all that. If he was going to leave anyway, the best she could hope was that he'd go as fast as he came.

Luke stomped along Main Street, determined to put as much distance between him and Anna as possible.

How could he have imagined Anna would let him back into their lives? Of course she wouldn't. She'd made her own life without him, and she didn't need or want him in it. Or in their son's life, either.

Still, he'd told her he'd stay, and he would. Giving up so easily would only confirm Anna's fears, give her more reason to mistrust him. He'd volunteer for the church renovations and find longer-term accommodation.

Help me to be patient, Lord. Help me to trust You'll make the way clear for whatever You want to happen.

Walking fast, he passed the motel and moved into quiet residential streets. He missed the physical labor of his job already. Full of restless energy he needed to work off, he kept on going. The houses thinned out and the yards got bigger as he reached the outskirts of town.

This street looked familiar. Had the town's sole cab driven him along here yesterday?

He stopped outside a big old Victorian, looking every year of its age. The shutters drooped, the paintwork peeled, the windows and gingerbread trim needed urgent TLC, like the old picket fence. Missing shingles suggested the roof leaked.

Then he recognized where he was. On auto-pilot, he'd walked to Anna's house. The last place he should be. If she found him here, she'd surely think he was stalking Josh. He should move on, fast.

Still, he lingered, looking around.

Anna denied she needed help, but her house sure did. Her art sales clearly didn't extend to covering repairs. He could do this for her if she'd let him. A couple of weeks' work and he'd have the place sound and watertight, at least.

While he stood at the gate, a small animal bolted past him, headed straight for the street. He pounced, grabbing the trailing leash before the critter ran into the path of an oncoming car.

Hooves clattered on the sidewalk as he jerked the animal to a halt just in time.

Luke looked down and blinked. Not a runaway puppy. He'd caught hold of a black and white piglet wearing a harness.

"Hi there, little fella." He wasn't quite sure how to pat a pig, so he scratched it behind one ear. That seemed to do the trick. The critter closed its small round eyes and relaxed, with what looked like a smile on its piggy face.

"Pattie!" a reedy voice shrieked. "Pattie, come back!"

Josh.

That same mechanical whirring Luke heard yesterday sounded, then Josh appeared, powering his electric wheelchair along the drive. Luke held the lead up so Josh could see it. The boy's worried frown changed to a smile.

Luke's breath choked. He couldn't stop a grin cracking his face, couldn't stop staring at Josh. Seeing the boy's twisted spine, wasted muscles, and contracted hands punched him in the solar plexus, even as his chest expanded with joy at this unexpected blessing.

His son.

This was his son.

CHAPTER FOUR

LUKE TRIED NOT TO GAWK at Josh, though he ached to take in every detail. Instead, he forced words past the pounding of his heart. "This your pig?"

As if he needed to ask. Stepping closer, he held out the lead.

"Thank you!" Josh beamed as he reached a crooked hand to take it. Luke wouldn't trade that smile from his son for a billionaire's bank balance.

The pig leapt into Josh's lap. "Bad girl," he scolded, stroking her head. The pig grinned, seeming proud of her unauthorized adventure. "You know you aren't allowed to run off. That's the second time this week."

As Josh fought to fasten Pattie's lead to the arm of his chair, Luke fought his own battle. Watching his son struggle with such a simple task shattered something inside him. But he pushed back his urge to help. He'd worked with enough kids to know Josh would want to do it himself.

And Anna lived with this, day after day. His heart twisted for them both.

With the lead clipped securely at last, Josh smiled up at him, eyes gleaming with curiosity behind round rimmed glasses. "You saved her life. Good thing you were there to catch her."

"A *God* thing. He has perfect timing." Anna wouldn't like it, but Luke couldn't see this meeting as anything but part of God's plan. He offered the boy his hand. "I'm Luke Tanner."

"This is Pattie Pork Pie. And I'm Josh Harrison." He took Luke's hand and awkwardly shook it.

Awe tingled through Luke. That hand was flesh of his flesh. The first moment he'd considered God might exist had been when Josh's newborn fingers clutched at his.

Now he knew, without any doubt.

A heavyset older man appeared from behind the house and puffed along the driveway.

"This is Uncle Rob. He lives next door, and helps me with my inventions," Josh piped. "Uncle Rob, this is Luke. Pattie ran away, but Luke caught her for me."

"Roberto Rodi," the neighbor creaked out, eying Luke dubiously. Then he turned to Josh. "You've got your pig safe. Thank the man and come inside. Your mom doesn't want you talking to people we don't know."

Josh stared at Luke, head to one side like a sparrow, a frown creasing his forehead. "I do know you, don't I? I'm sure I do."

Luke dragged in a sharp breath. This would be the perfect time to tell Josh he was his father. But he couldn't. Anna needed time to get her head around the idea he'd be part of their son's life. And they needed to plan to tell Josh together, not have him blurt it out.

He picked his way through a minefield of half-truths. "I knew your mom when she was at college, before you were born." He turned to the suspicious neighbor. "Mr. Rodi, Anna knows I'm in town."

The man didn't need to know she probably wanted to run him out of town, like her father would have done.

"Are you looking for Mom?" Josh asked. "She's not here. That's why Uncle Rob is here with me. Not that I need babysitting. I think I'm old enough to be left on my own. But Mom won't let me."

Luke shook his head. He wouldn't admit what he'd been doing at Josh's age. Alone most nights, with only the TV for company. Ramen for dinner if he could scrounge enough change. Never knowing when Mom would get home, or what state she'd be in when she did.

His side of the family didn't have a good track record when it came to parenting.

But Josh's trusting chatter with a stranger, as much as his disability, made Anna's precautions wise. "Isn't fourteen the legal age to be home on your own in this state?" he asked.

The older man nodded grimly.

Josh's eyes widened. "Mom never said it would be breaking the law. Okay, now I get it. We can't break the law. My Gramps was a Deputy. He put lawbreakers in jail." Pride rang in the boy's thin voice.

Luke's throat tightened, and he said nothing. Deputy Harrison would have gladly put *him* in jail.

"Outlaws go on the run. I'd have to go on the wheel." Josh grinned. "That could be a joke for my act. I was on the TV. Did you see me?"

"I sure did. You were great." A safe topic at last.

"Thanks! I really hope I can win the big prize — my own TV show. I'm practicing my act at the church fundraiser tonight. Will you come and watch?"

Josh wanted to see more of him. Luke's heart swelled. He couldn't refuse this gift. If Josh wanted him there, he'd be there. "Wouldn't miss it."

Before Luke could say more, an orange rust-bucket of a van clattered into the drive, stopping with a shuddering jolt. Anna jumped out. Her lips stretched in a tense smile that didn't meet her stormy eyes.

Luke stepped back from Josh and proffered an apologetic grimace. He'd invaded her turf, and she had every right to be annoyed. Last she knew, he'd agreed to wait and respect her timing. Now here he was, with their son.

"Josh, please go inside." She pointed to the house. "No talking to strangers."

"But Mom, he knows you. He's not a stranger."

"You need to get ready for Power Soccer. Now." Her voice held steel.

Josh groaned, but moved his hand on the control for his wheelchair. "See you, Luke. Thanks for your help."

Loss twanged at Luke, but he glued on a cheerful smile and waved as Josh trundled away.

Help Anna accept me being here please, Lord. Help her to accept I should play a role in our son's life.

She turned to her neighbor, who hovered watchfully, hands formed into meaty fists. "Roberto, thanks for staying with Josh. I'll take care of things now."

"You sure you're okay? I don't like to leave you with a man

27

hanging around, after what happened." The older man raised his chin, as if daring Luke to try anything.

Luke lifted his palms in a gesture of surrender. Provoking a confrontation was never wise. When the other man was six inches shorter and forty years his senior, it bordered on criminal. But he'd need to find out what Roberto meant.

If someone had threatened Anna... His jaw tightened.

"I'm fine." Anna smiled at her protector and waved her hands in a cutting gesture, telling him he could back down. "I do know him. He's safe."

Roberto left reluctantly, with a narrow-eyed glance at Luke.

As soon as he moved out of hearing range, Anna planted her hands on her hips and shook her head. "I told Roberto you were safe, but it doesn't feel that way. It feels like you betrayed me. You came to my home when you knew I was away. What did you tell Josh?" Emotion vibrated in her voice.

Her suspicion stung. "Nothing more than you said last night. That I knew you when you were in college. It wouldn't be fair to you to tell him the truth yet, when we agreed not to."

Lips twisted, she tilted her head back to meet his eyes. "You didn't worry about what was fair to me when you came here."

"I'm sorry." He waved his hands, taking in the driveway. "I didn't mean to walk this far. I was about to turn back when Josh's pig ran into the street. If I hadn't been here to catch her before the car did, she really *would* be pork patty."

Anger visibly deflating, Anna slumped, looked down, and scuffed the gravel with the tip of one sneaker. "Thanks for that," she muttered. "Josh would be devastated if anything happened to Pattie."

Luke put his hands behind his neck and stretched his head back, as much to stop himself reaching out to her as to pull the kinks out of his muscles.

All he could think of was how close she was, how the light floral scent of her shampoo filled his nostrils. The longing to gather her against him, bury his face in her hair, and kiss away whatever troubled her nearly overwhelmed him.

But what lay between them was too big for a kiss to fix. She'd slap his face hard enough to knock him into Sunday if he tried. Winning her trust again would take time.

Like building a house. Stick by stick. Brick by brick.

He filled his lungs and let the air go while he chose his words. "We need to decide together how and when we'll tell Josh the truth, and what role I'm to have in his life."

Anna scrubbed her hands over her face. "I know," she admitted, as if the words choked her. Her troubled gaze met his. "But I need to be sure you intend to stay. If Josh discovers who you are and you leave, he'll be shattered. I don't want him hurt."

"I do intend to stay. And I don't want Josh hurt, either." Mustering all his conviction, he injected it into his steady tone. Then he recalled a question he needed to ask. "What did your neighbor mean by 'after what happened'?"

Her lips tightened. "Nothing."

"Really? He seemed too worried for it to be nothing."

"Nothing *serious*. Some people see anyone on TV as public property. I had one or two persistent unwanted visitors as a result of *Talent Trek*. Marriage proposals, the works. And now I have you to deal with." Shaking her head, she loosed a long heavy breath, then spun on her heel and rushed toward the house.

Luke stared after her. To her, was he no more than another of those unwanted visitors?

Tension still vibrated through Anna hours later, as she stopped the van in the parking lot behind the old timber church. Exhausted, she longed to curl up in a quiet dark corner and pull the blankets over her head. Only for a week or two.

Even one evening would be good.

But tonight was not that evening. Josh had looked forward to this fundraiser for weeks.

She opened the back doors of the van and hauled Josh's wheelchair ramps into position with a grunt. Those things didn't get any lighter. Maybe someday she could afford a motorized ramp. Until then, no need for the gym.

Josh chattered non-stop while she unclicked his wheelchair locks. She tried to at least look as if she listened to him. Seeing him with Luke this afternoon rattled her more than she wanted to admit. The two of them looked so right together, Josh laughing with his father.

He wanted a dad so badly.

But Luke was a virtual stranger, who just happened to be the father of her son.

Telling herself that didn't stop the jump her traitor heart made when Luke was around, or quench the yearning for him she still felt.

Josh maneuvered his chair out of the van, and looked across to the playground, where his buddies clustered on bicycles and skateboards. "Can I go, Mom?"

Anna nodded. "Sure. But stay where I can see you, okay?"

Josh nodded, then took off toward his friends, who gathered around him. His high-pitched, excited voice carried across the lot, bragging about his winning goal at Power Soccer that afternoon. A genuine smile replaced the pinned-on plastic one she'd worn. If Josh was happy, her fatigue didn't matter.

She had to leave the situation with Luke in God's hands. Or at least try to.

After shoving the ramps back inside the van, she picked up her dessert bowl for tonight's auction, balancing it in the crook of her arm while she jiggled the key in the reluctant door lock.

"Let me help you." Luke's deep voice sounded right beside her. As he reached across to lift the heavy dish from its precarious perch, his fingertips brushed against her skin. The lightest of touches, yet enough to set her senses somersaulting.

She spun around to face him. Good thing he had a firm grip on the bowl, or it would lie smashed on the ground. Scattered and in pieces, like her senses. "Don't startle me like that! I had it."

Luke didn't need to know she leaned on the van door as much to support her wobbly legs as to keep it closed.

He smiled, crinkling the tanned skin around those deep blue eyes. "Why struggle when you don't have to?"

Her lips twisted. When would he get the message? "Because that's what I've had to do. And once you leave, that's what I'll have to do again."

Luke shook his head, and stared across the parking lot at Josh. Something in his gaze startled her. Protectiveness, tenderness, caring. He looked at Josh the way a father who loved his son did. The way he'd looked in that photo.

Maybe she could dare to trust him.

Maybe he wouldn't leave.

But it was all happening too fast. She needed to be sure.

Regret clouded his eyes when he turned back to her. "I'm sorry you've had to do so much on your own. I wanted to take care of you both." He sounded so warm, so sincere.

Old remembered feelings flooded her, unwanted and unbidden. She'd been so in love with him at eighteen. "I know. I wanted that too. But we could never have managed, not with a sick baby. Dad was right about that." Her words emerged as barely a whisper.

Luke's jaw tensed and his shoulders stiffened. He and Dad had never seen eye to eye. "Could be he was right, about me then. But I've grown up."

She crossed her arms over her chest. Her feelings for Luke had overwhelmed her sense of right and wrong once before. She couldn't regret Josh's conception, that would be too much like wishing him out of existence. But she needed a clearer mind now.

"I need to know what's best for Josh. That's all that matters. Not what we once felt for each other." Thankfully, her voice stayed firm. No trace of a wobble.

He nodded. "I don't want to rush you. I know you need time to decide you can trust me."

So he heard the words she hadn't said. It's too soon. Pinning on that falsely cheery smile again, she changed the subject. "So, why are you here?"

"Josh invited me to watch his act. I'll be worshiping here, anyway. And I plan to volunteer for the building work."

So he really did plan to stay. Honesty compelled her to admit part of her wanted that, as much for her sake as Josh's. But a bigger part of her wished he'd leave town now, before he made their lives even more complicated.

How would she keep the truth from Josh till she felt sure of Luke? And how could she control her unruly emotions, when she'd be seeing him so often? She shivered at the thought.

"We should sit in your van to talk. You're cold." His warm hand took her elbow. The touch burned through her thin cardigan.

She pulled away, tugging the cardigan around herself. Luke shook her to the core, not the cool spring evening. "Not now. I have things to do."

Luke raised his eyebrows. "Things more important than discussing Josh?"

Unable to lie to him, she shook her head. Important things, like getting away from him, as far and as fast as possible. His nearness had her head spinning.

"We do need to talk about this sometime." He smiled. "How many weeks will it take to convince you that I'm not going anywhere?"

"I'm not the same trusting girl you remember. Too much has happened." Her voice rang strong, determined, like the woman she wanted to be.

Then she spoiled the effect by shivering again.

Luke rolled his eyes heavenward and perched the bowl on the roof of the van. "You are cold. Take this." He slipped off his old brown leather jacket and held it out to her. "I can see how me turning up like this is hard for you. But would you try meeting me half-way? Even quarter-way would be good."

Anna's heart hiccupped. Unfair that he looked so good in the white cotton button down shirt he wore. Shaking her head, she lifted her hands like stop signs. His jacket came loaded with too many memories.

Luke stood, jacket dangling from his hand, his warm gaze fixed on her.

Was he remembering the night she'd first worn his jacket, too?

CHAPTER FIVE

LETTING MEMORIES OF THEIR PAST closeness affect things now was a mistake. Despite that, Anna couldn't help hoping. That Josh could have the loving father he wanted. That she could share the job of parenting him. That Luke would stay this time.

But her trust had taken too many knocks. Luke leaving. Josh's diagnosis. Mom and Dad dying.

Each time, something died in her too.

Luke just stood there, holding out his jacket, lips twisted in a rueful smile. "Why be cold when you don't have to be? I won't think it means you're weak. You've raised Josh on your own, so you must be strong."

Something in the way he asked, rather than demanded, melted her resistance.

She wasn't sure she couldn't trust him, any more than she trusted her clunker of a van not to break down at the most inconvenient times. But none of that mattered when Luke looked at her with warmth in his eyes, his smile crinkling them at the corners.

She took the jacket and slid her arms into the sleeves. His body heat lingered in the fabric lining and seeped into her skin. It felt as intimate as Luke slipping his own arms around her. Her choked breath drew in his masculine aroma of worn leather and soap.

After all these years it shouldn't feel so achingly familiar, yet it was.

The night they first met he'd wrapped her in this jacket when he took her home to her dorm, perched behind him his motorbike.

Sadness swept her, for all she'd hoped she and Luke would have. Lifting her eyes to his, she loosed a long breath. "I *did* try to contact you, when I found out Josh was ill. But you'd gone."

She wanted to sound like she had it all together.

Instead, she sounded forlorn.

He glanced down, but not before she saw the grief and loss shadowing his eyes.

She knew that look. She saw it in her mirror whenever she forgot to straighten her expression first.

Rubbing his fingers over the bump in his nose, he sucked in a noisy breath before replying. "I'm sorry I wasn't there for you, Anna. I thought you didn't want me in your life." His throat worked as he swallowed. "It hurt, knowing you wanted Josh adopted, brought up by strangers instead of us."

The raw honesty in his words broke something in her. She pressed both fists to her stinging eyes for a moment. "I had to choose. Go with you or do what Dad wanted. Maybe I chose wrong. But you never wrote, never contacted me. You disappeared out of our lives, like we meant nothing to you."

Her little-girl whimper gave away how deeply he'd wounded her.

Luke held out his hands. She shook her head. The emotions battling inside her were too strong. She couldn't risk physical contact.

His arms dropped to his sides. "I did write. After the first three letters were returned, I figured you didn't want to hear from me."

"I never got any letters." She folded her arms and lifted her chin, knowing she'd accused him of lying. Retreating into defensiveness was safer than longing to believe him.

"I sent them here, to your home address." His voice held quiet dignity. "Your parents?"

She yanked in a jerky painful breath. Dad had hated Luke, been furious with him. And with her, too, for shaming him. But she'd never imagined he'd take her mail.

Wasn't that a felony?

Regardless, she knew Luke wasn't lying.

"Dad could have been angry enough to do that," she admitted. "He'd think he was protecting me. I assumed you'd forgotten us."

"I never forgot you, or Josh." Her heart flipped at the sincerity shining in his eyes.

Then the whir of Josh's approaching wheelchair reminded her of the reality. Time to stop behaving and thinking like the foolish girl she'd been, and act like the woman she had to be. A mature, responsible mother, whose son's needs came first.

Straightening her shoulders, she put on a bright smile for Josh.

He only had eyes for his father, twisting his neck to beam up at Luke. "You came!"

"Wouldn't miss it, cowboy." Luke's smile held such sweet tenderness. He placed a hand on Josh's shoulder.

Seeing them side by side, she gasped. They looked so alike. It wouldn't take people long to realize the connection. Somehow, she needed to keep them apart, until she had a chance to talk to Josh.

Their son turned his head, peering at them both. Curiosity gleamed in his eyes. He wouldn't fail to notice she was wearing Luke's jacket.

She rushed into action. "We need to find Pastor Dan and discuss your act, Josh. Here's your jacket back, Luke. Thanks for lending it to me." She shrugged it off and thrust it at him.

"But I want to talk to Luke," Josh protested.

"No! We need to go." Her words came out louder than she intended.

She turned the key in the van's lock, grateful it worked this time, and grabbed the dessert bowl from its perch on the roof.

They needed to get away from Luke, and stay away for the rest of the evening. She didn't want Josh to know about him yet, and no one else must guess, either.

Luke's return sent her life spiraling out of her control, and she couldn't do a thing about it.

Anna's maneuvers to keep him away from Josh amused and frustrated Luke in equal measure. Buzzing around the crowded church hall, she appeared at Josh's side whenever the boy as much as twitched an eye in his direction.

She was being a good mother, protecting their son like a mama bear. He wouldn't wish her any different.

As long as she didn't take too long to trust him.

His eyes sought her, standing across the room beside the deputy. In a pretty blue-green dress, with her hair loosely curled, she barely looked older than she did in the photo he carried over his heart. A few faint lines around her eyes when she smiled. An added maturity and confidence.

Anna's brand of beauty didn't fade.

Her laughter rang out as she smiled up at the lawman. Possessiveness he had no right to feel arced through him. Pushing out a painful breath, he forced his clenched hands to relax, along with his stiff jaw.

A ginger-haired man in his mid-thirties approached, extending a hand the size of a ham. "I'm Dan Waters, the pastor. Glad to meet you. New in town?" The pastor's hearty handshake gave a sense of contained strength.

Luke blinked. The stocky man looked more like a boxer. Unlike his own bumpy nose, Dan's had been steamrollered, not just broken.

"Luke Tanner. I arrived yesterday, but plan to settle here. This fundraiser, it's for the church repairs?"

"Yep." Dan nodded. "The roof needs replacing. We'll need do as much of the work as we can ourselves. We hope to pay only for the materials and a builder to lead the team."

Luke whistled at the figure Dan mentioned. "I'm out of touch with U.S. prices. Where I've been working, we could build a whole village for that."

"Looks like our Finance Committee is out of touch with U.S. prices, too." Dan's lips thinned. "The amount we'd allocated is nowhere near enough."

"I may be able to help. Have you heard of House the World?"

Five minutes and a cellphone call to Larry later, Dan gave him a solid slap on the back, then stepped onto the makeshift stage. As he tapped the microphone, the chatter in the room quieted.

A broad smile split Dan's freckled face. "Welcome to our fundraiser! Whether you've come for the entertainment, the dessert auction, or out of good neighborly spirit, I'm glad to see you, and hope you enjoy the evening. Let's begin by thanking the Lord for bringing us together, and asking his blessing on us."

Luke bowed his head, his heart full. He had so much to give thanks for. As the pastor ended his prayer with a loud Amen, he echoed it.

Dan spoke again. "We're all here to give to the building fund, through time, cash, or prayer support, and I'm pleased to report that a newcomer to town has started our night of giving in a big way." His contagious grin broke out again as he gestured toward Luke. "Please welcome Luke Tanner, an experienced building project manager, who's gifting us his expertise. He'll stay in the church house with me while he leads the work. Luke, come up on stage."

Over the ripples of appreciation, a gasp sounded across the room. Luke's head snapped around. Anna stared at him, wide-eyed and open-mouthed in dismay.

Why such alarm that he'd found a way to stay here? Disappointment twisted in his stomach. She really must want him to leave.

Josh, beside her, gave a wide gap-toothed smile and a shoulder-high victory punch. No need to guess there. He returned his son's delighted smile with a thumbs up.

Making his way to the stage, Luke passed close enough to Anna to reach out to her. He didn't, though he longed to. Dan asked Luke to introduce himself, and handed him the mic.

Thankfully, pitching House the World projects to potential backers taught him how to speak in public. But this time, he forgot the rules. Instead of keeping his gaze moving around the room, making eye contact with as many audience members as possible, he kept looking at just two people.

Anna, her face unreadable. And Josh, whose hopeful grin tore Luke in two.

As he left the stage, Josh spoke to him. "My act's next. Will you watch?"

Josh really did want him around. Gratitude flooded Luke's chest, warm and sweet. "Wouldn't be anywhere else, cowboy."

But Anna didn't even glance his way. That softening he'd imagined out in the parking lot had vanished. "Time to get ready, Josh," she said.

Josh maneuvered his wheelchair in front of the steps up to the stage.

"No ramp?" Luke didn't want to ask out loud if Josh could manage it. Those few shallow steps would be daunting as Everest to someone with mobility issues.

"We tried, but there's simply not enough space. These old

buildings weren't constructed with disabled access in mind." A what-business-is-it-of-yours note edged her words.

His lips tightened. His son's well-being was his business.

"I can manage," Josh declared, with only the tiniest wobble. "I've been practicing at home." He grasped the metal rail on the wall and strained to haul himself upright, face scrunched with the effort.

A boy his age needed his independence, but Luke couldn't stand by. He jumped onto the stage and planted himself one step in front of Josh. "Can I give you a hand, cowboy?"

Josh cocked his head to one side to look up at Luke, then nodded uncertainly.

Luke turned from Josh to the chair waiting for him on the stage, right next to the steps, assessing the problem.

Help me do this right, please, Lord.

"I need you to trust me enough to hang onto me and not the rail. Can you do that?"

Josh's nod this time looked way less tentative.

Luke leaned forward, hooked his arms under Josh's armpits and around his back, and lifted enough to take most of his weight off his legs. He could carry him to the chair without breaking a sweat, but he wouldn't embarrass Josh like that.

Josh straightened, letting go his white knuckle grip on the rail and grasping Luke's arms instead. He smiled. "Let's do it!"

His son trusted him. Pride expanded Luke's heart till he could explode with joy.

Now he had to prove himself worthy of that trust.

Anna's nails dug into her palms as she watched Luke do for Josh what she couldn't. When he was little, she'd carried him when he couldn't walk, but he'd grown too tall and heavy for her.

Josh stubbornly rejected her suggestion to let Connor or Dan help him, insisting he'd do it himself. Then he let Luke do it.

But Luke didn't seem to pull and drag him the way Connor did. He supported Josh while the boy took his own slow, unsteady steps, safe in his father's strong hold. Step by laborious step, Josh made it to the stage.

Luke settled him in the chair, and they high fived.

No one seeing them side by side could doubt they were father and son. She risked a glance behind her. Tabby Whytecliff's eyes shone like a cat's when toying with a mouse. Just what they didn't need — the town's most determined gossip figuring out the truth before she told Josh herself.

Worse, Josh obviously decided the man was his hero. All through his performance, instead of looking to her for approval as he usually did, his eyes stayed fixed on Luke. Anna rubbed at the tears scalding her eyelids.

She never cried, and now she'd done it twice in one evening.

But the apprehension jangling her nerves didn't stop her awareness of Luke. Every cell in her body was sensitized to his nearness.

He helped Josh off the stage at the end of the comedy routine, and stayed by their side through the rest of the show. As soon as the entertainment ended, she made an all-too-obvious excuse to haul a protesting Josh across the room. His teacher, Tim, talking to the pretty new school receptionist, didn't look too happy at her interruption, either.

Everyone seemed to be watching her, especially the folk who'd been cold and disapproving when she'd come home from college pregnant. This evening couldn't get any worse.

Then, in the dessert auction, Luke and Connor started a bidding war over her Snickers pudding.

She cringed as they faced off across the room, gunslingers shooting bids at each other. Along with everyone else, her head swiveled from one to the other as bidding climbed to a ridiculous level. Each man seemed equally determined not to let the other win.

Neither of them had any reason. Connor knew she didn't want to be more than friends. And Luke knew she didn't want him back in her life.

When bids reached near to a week's salary for a deputy in Clearwater County, Connor shrugged and conceded defeat.

Every eye in the room focused on her. Her hot face might just spontaneously combust. If only she could snatch up the dessert bowl and a spoon and run somewhere no one could watch her gobble the entire pudding. Though she doubted there was enough chocolate on the planet to make this feel better.

Eyebrows halfway up his forehead, mouth hanging open, Josh

stared across the room at Luke. "He must really like Snickers pudding."

Anna could only nod. "Guess so." She hardly managed to squeak the words.

The man must be crazy. Certifiably nuts. Insane. How could he attract even more attention to them? She didn't dare peek in the direction of Tabby and her cronies. Especially when they started circling Luke like vultures.

"I think he likes you, not Snickers pudding," Josh declared. "Was he your boyfriend in college?"

She didn't answer, but Josh didn't seem to notice her silence. He gazed at Luke, eyes thoughtful. "If you want to date him now, I don't mind. He could come to the father-son stuff at school and do Scouts with me, like the other guys' dads."

The wistfulness in his voice scraped Anna raw. Luke still had his bad-boy charm, and it worked just as well on her son as it had on her. He'd totally won Josh over, in less than a day.

She glanced across the room at Luke, and her breath caught "Don't get too hopeful. We don't know how long he'll be staying." Her words were as much a warning for herself as for Josh.

Josh kept staring at Luke.

Then he turned to her, accusation burning in his eyes. "Mom, I'm not stupid. Luke knew you before I was born. He has hair just like mine. His eyes are the same color too. If you won't tell me the truth, I'll ask him."

Inevitable as a train wreck about to happen, she knew what he'd do next. Her frantic "No, Josh," went unheeded. The crowd parted like the Red Sea as he scooted his wheelchair across the room at top speed.

Luke squatted beside him with a wide smile. "Hey, cowboy. Want a share of the pudding? It looks good."

Josh didn't smile. His face was the most serious she'd seen it.

Anna didn't pray as much as she should, but she prayed now.

Don't let him say it. Don't let him say it. Don't let him say it.

She closed her eyes as his words fell like stones in a pool of sudden silence.

"Luke, I have to know. Are you my father?"

CHAPTER SIX

LUKE GULPED, STRUGGLING TO DRAG in a breath. Josh's question sucked all the air out of the room.

Truth time, far sooner than any of them were prepared for.

The sensation of so many watching eyes prickled across his skin. Telling Josh he was his father wasn't something he'd planned on doing with an audience.

That was the problem. He hadn't planned. He'd come charging into their lives like some caped crusader SuperDad, and fallen flat on his face. At least, he'd hoped when they told Josh the truth, it would be the three of them together, somewhere quiet and peaceful.

Not a crowded hall with most of the town staring at them.

Josh leaned forward in his wheelchair, biting his lip, hands white knuckled on his chair's arm rests. His eyes pleaded for an answer.

The silence stretched, so solid and thick Luke could almost reach out and touch it.

His throat tightened until he couldn't speak, even if he had a clue what to say. He tugged at his shirt collar, but it still choked. He'd told Anna he'd respect her wishes and wait, but this wasn't about him and Anna. This was about Josh and what he needed.

Some secrets had to be told.

Swallowing hard, he glanced at Anna. With her face crumpled and hands clasped under her chin, she looked a little girl hoping all this would go away if she closed her eyes tight enough. He wanted to hug her, tell her it would be okay, take away her fear.

But he couldn't. All he could do was tell Josh the truth, even though she wasn't ready. He'd been willing to wait, but now the choice of time and place was out of their hands. Guilt coiled like barbed wire in his guts.

Luke saw in Josh's eyes which answer he wanted. Josh wanted him to be his dad. The blessing of it warmed him, glowing like a fire in his chest, releasing some of the tightness lodged there since Josh lobbed that hand grenade of a question his way. Josh needed and deserved an honest reply. He wouldn't take that hope away by hedging and delaying.

Josh stared up at them, and the spark of hope in his blue eyes dulled. He sighed and slumped in his wheelchair.

Luke looked to Anna, praying she'd understand. They had to do it, now. Her lips were pressed together tight, arms wrapped around her chest, but she nodded.

He squatted next to Josh's chair to meet his son on his level, then poured all the love he could into his smile. Josh's eyes still held confusion and anger, but a tentative, hopeful, shadow of a smile flickered on his lips.

"This wasn't the way we hoped to tell you, Josh, but yes, I'm your father."

He wasn't sure what response he'd hoped for from Josh, but he didn't get it. The emotion drained out of Josh's face, leaving it blank and expressionless. No hint what the kid was thinking or feeling. He'd turned so far inward it felt as if he wasn't there at all.

Startled, Luke looked to Anna. She didn't respond, her attention fixed on Josh.

All Luke could do was hope, and pray.

Lord, let Josh be okay with this. Help me be a good father to him. Please, show us how we can be a family.

Anna bit her lip as she waited for Josh to respond. The pain reminded her not to intervene, no matter how much she wanted to.

He'd blanked out. She'd seen it before when he had to deal with something too big to handle, like serious discussions at doctor's appointments or after his hamster died. The doctor explained that he needed time to process, and had to be allowed to do it. No interruption, however long it took.

She couldn't speak, could barely breathe, could only stand watching him.

Up on stage, Dan's voice boomed out. "Let's not forget the reason we're here, the building work. I'm calling for volunteers to sign up."

Despite his attempts at distraction, she heard the whispers, felt the eyes watching them. Something inside her shriveled. Her private life was public knowledge again, just like when she'd first come home expecting Josh.

Now it would start all over again. The silent disapproval. The sideways looks. The whispers that stopped when she walked into a room.

A sigh edged past the stone-hard worry in her chest. Josh had to be told about Luke eventually, yes. But not this way, completely unprepared, with most of Sweetapple Falls looking on. Like so many other things in his life, this was one more thing she couldn't protect him from, no matter how much she wanted to.

All she'd ever wanted was to be a good mother for him. Tonight, she'd failed spectacularly.

When Josh asked, Luke had no choice but to answer honestly. It should be perfect. Their son wanted a dad, and now he had one. Ready and willing.

Still, losing any choice over that decision flooded her with panic.

Luke shoved a hand through his thick hair and gestured toward Josh. Apology clouded the brightness of his eyes, so like Josh's the resemblance twisted her heart. His furrowed brow asked an unspoken question.

The craziest impulse to smooth away those deep lines hit her. His concern for Josh warmed her heart. He wanted what was best for their son, as much as she did.

His concern for *her* touched her too, far deeper than she wanted.

With a reassuring smile and raised hands warning him to do nothing, she tried to tell him to wait, that it would pass. He gave a grateful half smile in return, then bowed his head.

Maybe God would respond to Luke's prayers. It seemed He didn't listen to hers.

As Josh stayed withdrawn, longer than he'd ever done before, staying quiet and doing nothing became harder and harder to bear. She shifted from foot to foot. Luke's worried glances told her the wait was just as hard for him.

Escalating whispers around them, throat clearing and shuffling of feet suggested others were becoming anxious, too. Any second now, some well-meaning person would step in to interfere, and she'd almost certainly snap at them.

At last, Josh's hands clutched convulsively on the arms of his chair and he blinked. The breath she'd been holding escaped in an whoosh.

Thank You, God!

Luke grinned like someone handed him his dreams on a plate. She couldn't help smiling in return.

But Josh remained silent. His gaze shifted from her to Luke, then back to her, but his face gave away nothing of what he felt or thought.

The need to do something or say something to help him, no matter how inadequate, consumed her. "Josh, I'm sorry," she murmured, reaching out to him.

His expression hardened, stopped her dead. Pest exterminators examined cockroaches with more warmth. This wasn't a childish tantrum, flaring up then passing. This went deeper, scarily adult on his child's face, raising goose bumps on her arms and chilling her all the way through. She shivered, wrapping her arms around herself.

Nothing in her twelve years with Josh had prepared her for his icy rage. Looking to Luke, she silently begged him to help.

"Josh?" Luke asked, resting a hand on Josh's arm. "Talk to me, cowboy. Okay?"

Josh pulled his arm away and swiveled his head to glare at Luke. "Where have you been all my life? And why didn't you tell me sooner?" His voice bristled, shrill with outrage. Emotion twisted his small face. "Are you ashamed of me? Is that why you stayed away so long?"

"No! It's my fault." The words ripped out of her. That Josh could jump to that hurtful conclusion buried hooks deep in her heart and tore it right out of her chest. "He wanted to tell you yesterday. I asked him not to. He thought you'd been adopted as a baby, and only discovered three days ago that I couldn't let you go."

She'd wanted to protect Josh by giving a half-truth on Friday after Luke came to the door. And look at the results. Dad had been right.

Evading the truth was as bad as telling a lie.

Josh was hurting now, way more than if she'd told him the truth right away.

Her gaze collided with Luke's. His eyes mirrored the confusion she felt, and their shared concern for their son. Dragging in a painful breath, she stepped toward Josh. She longed for the chance to explain, apologize, hug his pain away, like she did when he'd been younger and had a boo-boo.

But Josh's hand scrabbled on his chair control. He backed away, holding up a thin hand to stop them. His eyes glittered, bright with tears. "Leave me alone, both of you! Especially you, Mom." The accusing glance he threw at her cut deep.

"Josh, no!"

He ignored her, steering toward the door at top speed, scattering the audience so avidly pretending not to listen.

Never in her life had she felt so useless, so helpless.

Every eye in the place seemed to bore into her as she hurried across the airless hall after Josh, careful to avoid meeting anyone's eyes. With Failure tattooed across her soul, she didn't need to see it confirmed by judgmental stares.

Luke's footsteps sounded close behind on the wooden floor.

Outside in the parking lot, she gulped the cool fresh air and scanned for Josh in the pools of lamplight piercing the darkness. There. In the playground, next to the slide she'd lifted him onto again and again and again when he was younger.

His head turned at the sound of her feet crunching on the gravel, and he swiveled his chair away from her. Narrow hunched shoulders warned her to keep her distance.

She took a step toward him, then stopped. Her desire to fix things, to be the good mother she so desperately wanted Josh to have, battled with the risk of being exactly the sort of smother mother he didn't need. Frustration churned her stomach.

While she hesitated, Luke caught her arm and gently swung her around to face him. "You okay?" he asked, gazing down at her, face creased in concern.

A jerk of her arm freed it from his grip. "Of course I'm not okay. My son is more upset than I've ever seen him, and my private life will be next week's biggest news topic at the diner."

Her angry words weren't fair. But the more she bolstered her antagonism, the easier it was to resist him. Resist the way her senses danced at his nearness, despite her anxiety for Josh.

She didn't need or want this awareness of his touch she couldn't even begin to suppress.

Luke glanced toward Josh, and then focused his gaze on her. Caring and compassion emanated from him.

Uneasiness skittered along her nerves. The understanding in his eyes was too much. She looked away, desperate to avoid drowning in those blue depths.

"I'm sorry," Luke said. "Josh needed to know, but I didn't mean for it to happen this way. I'll do whatever I can to make things right."

Listening hard for a hint of insincerity, anything she could use to defend herself against the flare of hope that this time he meant it, all she heard was a genuine desire to make amends. Like a wave threatening to pull her under, sadness swept her. Grief for the lost years, for what they could have had.

The one time she'd swum in the ocean, the current carried her out too far. The constant effort to keep her head above water when her feet couldn't touch the bottom terrified her. This felt the same. Way out of her depth, in over her head, and tired of treading water. If she stopped fighting, she'd drown. But exhaustion overwhelmed her.

All she wanted to do was let go, surrender, give up the fight.

"It doesn't have to be this hard," Luke said, as if he'd guessed her thoughts. "I'm here to help you. Why not let me?"

For a moment, longing to stop struggling and trust that the life-raft Luke offered would keep her afloat flooded her. But she could barely trust God since Mom and Dad died, so how could she trust Luke?

If she trusted him and he left, she'd sink like a stone.

And who'd take care of Josh then?

Luke should have guessed Anna wouldn't accept his support. Not yet.

For a moment, she'd been ready to give in and trust him. It showed, in the slump of her shoulders, the sigh that escaped her drooping lips, her softened expression. Then she straightened her shoulders and shook her head, the sudden movement making her long hair swing. As she gazed across the parking lot at Josh, silence stretched between them.

Chances were he'd never regain her trust, let alone her love. Once she knew how he'd messed up after he left, he'd be lucky if she let him within a mile of her. His impulsive, hurt-fueled mistakes after he left them in the hospital backed him into a corner with only two choices. Jail, or House the World.

Because of that, he hadn't been there when she needed his help. When Josh developed health problems. When her parents died.

Lord, how did I get it so wrong? Was coming to Sweetapple Falls Your will, or only my own?

From one breath to the next, sureness filled him. God brought him back to be the father Josh wanted, and to support Anna too.

She sagged as she stared at Josh's stubbornly turned back, and scrubbed her hands over her face. "I need to go to him."

He'd give anything to take the misery from her eyes and the hopelessness from her voice. He wanted to go to Josh too, but experience with kids on the building projects told him to wait.

Saying that to Anna could put him on shaky ground. While he'd been working with other men's kids, she'd had twelve years caring for their son alone.

What did he know about fatherhood? All he'd learned about being a dad came from watching the guys on the building teams with their children, and from one good foster father, who he'd betrayed.

The fear he wouldn't be good enough sank its teeth into him, deep and hard. He straightened his shoulders, fighting down the fear. He wouldn't let Anna and Josh down.

"Kids his age need to cool off by themselves sometimes." He offered the words tentatively, more a question than a statement, praying he was right about how to handle things. Josh wasn't like other kids. That withdrawal thing in the hall nearly gave him a heart attack.

Anna raised her head, a hint of hope sparking in her eyes.

"He knows we're here. He'll show us when he's ready to talk." All the confidence and reassurance he could muster surged into his voice. "When it's time, we'll go to him. We'll deal with this together."

He wanted her to hear his willingness to be there for her, as well as Josh.

"We didn't do it together before. You weren't there when I

needed you." Her words could have been bitter. Instead, she sounded like a child seeking reassurance.

Regret ached deep inside him. Words wouldn't comfort her. Only time and faith and his steady support could restore her trust. He wanted to hug her, hold her, make her see that he'd stay. If he could kiss all the anger and pain and sadness away, maybe the love she'd once had for him would return. Maybe they'd get another chance to be a family.

Fat chance. This was real life, not a fairy tale.

Could he tell her about his past? Get all the secrets out, and start over, clear and clean?

As he opened his mouth to speak, the idea sickened his stomach. They needed to get through the fallout from Josh's bombshell before he dropped any more. Digging into the past now wouldn't give her the reassurance she wanted. It would only make things worse.

The Deputy hadn't raised his daughter to tolerate mistakes like his.

"I'm sorry. I wish I'd been there." Every day since he found out about Josh, he'd regretted the foolish choices he'd made. No do-overs, unless God gave him a time machine.

For a moment, her gaze collided with his, full of wistful yearning.

He reached towards her, his hand hovering in the space between them, a silent plea for forgiveness. "God gave me a second chance. Will you?" His pulse pounded in his throat as he waited for her response, willing her hand to move towards his.

It lifted a little. Then she turned away, shaking her head. "I know Josh wants his father, but I can't turn back time just like that, and pretend we're eighteen again." Her voice shook slightly.

His hand dropped to his side. "I have all those years missing from your lives to make up for, and I'll do it." The rightness of it hit him. It wasn't only about being a father to Josh. It was about Anna and what she needed, too. "Anything you want, ask me. Financial support, driving Josh places, helping with his homework, fixing up your house and car. Even if all you want is someone to bring round some take-out because you're too tired to cook. I'll be here for you as well as Josh."

Whatever it took to be a father to Josh and prove to Anna she could trust him again, he'd do it. A simple promise, serious as a marriage vow.

A vow he meant with all his heart.

CHAPTER SEVEN

ANNA EYED LUKE.

He didn't seem upset by her refusal to take his hand. Instead, he smiled at her, open and accepting. She recognized something in his attitude toward her, and in how he'd dealt with Josh. A strength and determination he'd lacked in the past.

Maybe he had changed. Maybe, it wasn't just words.

But could she take the chance? Around him, she felt like a weak and vulnerable girl again. She'd worked too hard at getting strong and independent after losing Mom and Dad to want to depend on anyone else again. Even Luke.

Especially Luke.

The hum of Josh's wheelchair carried across the parking lot. At last she could go to him.

She rushed to the playground, Luke's footsteps echoing behind her. He'd moved his chair to the small teeter-totter, lifting it an inch with his foot and letting it drop with a thud. She knew how much that small effort must cost him.

He scowled at her, his face pale and pinched in the dim light.

Worry erased her tentative smile. "Josh?" she asked.

"Why didn't you tell me? You knew how much I wanted a dad."

His glare sliced into her, leaving her unable to string two words together. Knees wobbling, she sank onto a bench. She didn't know how to reach him through the intensity of his rage. His temper normally calmed as quickly as a summer storm. Not this time.

And her insistence on the ostrich approach landed them here.

Luke squatted beside Josh. "Your mom and I are sorry we upset you. You caught us by surprise. We'd planned to tell you, but not so soon." He smiled, with enough reassurance to make her heart flip over with hope.

Josh's tense expression didn't change. "Mom wanted to keep you secret. I know it." He said mom like a curse.

Anna crumpled. She couldn't quite read the look Luke threw her. Apology, desire to help, caring? His understanding warmed and lifted her, despite her worry for Josh.

Luke's forehead creased as he exhaled audibly. "You're right. Your mom did ask me not to tell you yet. Not to keep secrets from you, but because she loves you and doesn't want you to get hurt."

Josh shook his head. "How would telling me hurt?" His scrutiny swiveled back to her, pinning her like a collector pinned a butterfly. "Why did you want to stop me knowing my dad?"

She bit her lip, struggling to find words to explain, to wipe the distress from Josh's face. There were none, but she had to say something. "Josh, I'm sorry. I did what I thought was best for you."

His lip curled and hot color flared in his cheeks. "Stop treating me like I'm a little kid. Just because I'm in this" — he raised a twisted arm, and dropped it against the side of his wheelchair — "you think you can keep me a kid forever. Well you can't."

He seemed less and less a child with every word.

Her throat felt so tight she didn't trust herself to speak. Of course she wanted to keep him a child. What mother told her son might die before his teens wouldn't? Tonight, he'd catapulted into adolescence, and she couldn't do a thing to stop it.

She was losing him. The knowledge ached in her like a broken bone.

But this was about Josh. His needs, not hers.

She'd disappointed him and betrayed his trust, when he needed to rely on her. The only way to put things right between them was to admit she'd messed up.

Luke spoke first. "Don't blame your mom. She had her reasons for not telling you sooner. I wasn't good father material when you were born. That's why your Gramps made her break up with me. She wanted to wait and be sure I'd stay around."

He looked down, rubbing that bump on his nose. This had to be tough for him, exposing his own shortcomings to protect her from Josh's blame.

She squeezed her eyes shut to stop the threatening tears. One hand lifted to press on the tight ball of discomfort in her chest.

Josh's face creased in his figuring-stuff-out frown. "But why would you leave now?" His thin chest rose and fell in a sigh. "Because of this?" He waved one arm, taking in his chair and his twisted body. "Because you don't want to be my dad when I'm like this?" He hunched like a beaten dog expecting a kick.

She and Luke both reached toward him. Luke's hand connected first, resting firm and strong on Josh's arm.

Her hand dropped back into her lap. Josh didn't want her touch. But she couldn't let him believe Luke didn't want him. It had killed something in her to lose her own dad's love.

Words rushed from her mouth. "He wanted to stay and be your dad when you were a baby. He only left after Gramps insisted I had to let you be adopted."

Puzzlement creased Josh's face. "But I wasn't adopted. If I was, I'd have a different Dad and Mom, wouldn't I?"

"I didn't want to let you go. Then when we found out you were ill, and the doctor said you might not live long, Gramps agreed you could stay with us. By then, Luke had gone away."

Through her concern for Josh, the knowledge that Luke hadn't truly loved her clawed at her heart. If he'd wanted her, not just their baby, surely he would have stayed even after Josh was adopted.

"Like your mom said, I didn't know you were sick. Knowing that now doesn't change how proud I am of my son." Emotion rasped in Luke's voice. Reaching into his pocket, he pulled out a tattered and yellowed plastic-covered photo, then handed it to Josh. "I've carried this the whole time I've been away, and prayed for you every day since I became a Christian."

She peeked at what Josh held. Their one "family" photo, the one the nurse had taken in the hospital. The same one she kept hidden in her wardrobe.

Josh glanced from Luke to her, and back to the picture. "This is you and Mom, right? And the baby, that's me?"

"It's you." Luke's smile melted her.

She willed Josh to melt too. To smile back, show he understood he wasn't the reason Luke left.

Josh didn't smile. He frowned at Luke, but a puzzled frown, with no sign of his earlier rage. "So why didn't you come back sooner?"

"I thought you'd have another family. I only realized the truth when I saw you on TV. I came here straight away." He looked to the ground. When he raised his head, tears glinted in his eyes.

She'd seen Luke cry only once before, the day Josh was born. Pressing on that lump in her chest didn't make it shift. She had to swallow, hard.

Josh seemed to be holding his breath, waiting for Luke to continue.

"With your mom's permission, I want us to spend some time together. Is that okay?" Luke threw a quick glance her way, but she knew the question was Josh's to answer.

No matter how hard it was for her, she wouldn't deny him his father.

Josh's gaze stayed tense and assessing, fixed on Luke. "You're really staying? You won't go away?"

"I'm staying." Luke gazed at his son, strong and steady. "If you want me to."

Josh smiled at last. He leaned toward Luke, more excited than she'd ever seen him, Christmas and Easter and his birthday all at once. "I want you to be my dad."

Anna let loose a long sigh. Josh was happy. That was all that mattered.

Joy lit Luke's face. Like the first time he'd held Josh, he looked as if he held the whole universe cradled in his arms and the wonder of it bowled him over. The longing to put her arms around them both as she'd done then swelled within her.

Then Josh turned toward her, his expression hardening. "Mom, can he?" His voice carried a let-him-or-else warning that tore at her.

If only she could say no, protect Josh from the disappointment that would knock him flat if Luke left them. But the possibility of Luke leaving was in the future. Josh's distress right now if she refused was a certainty.

"Sure," she said. She couldn't do anything to take away Josh's happiness. His future was too fragile.

Her son turned away from her as if she didn't exist, lifting an arm to high five Luke, his frail hand pressed against Luke's tanned capable one.

She couldn't hold him any longer. The knowledge filled her chest, cold and heavy and suffocating. Josh had the father he wanted, and everything had changed. He'd never need her in the same way again. One step nearer losing him.

And Luke was now an inescapable part of her life.

The next morning, Luke strolled the sunny tree-lined streets, praying for guidance. Last night, he'd upset Josh, and exposed Anna to gossip and scrutiny. They'd face more of the same today in church.

Most important was that Josh knew the truth now, knew his father cared. And though reluctant, Anna accepted and agreed to him being in their son's life. The thought lifted his heart.

He had contact with his son, and he had a job to do.

Arriving at the town's historical church, he ran an assessing eye over it. The small-steepled blue clapboard building and its white trim looked sound enough, but boards and shingles could hide problems. He'd size up the work properly tomorrow. So far, it looked like a project he could manage with volunteer crew.

He whispered a prayer of thanks. The church needing a contractor right when he got to town must surely be God's doing.

An already familiar rattle signaled Anna's van approaching. Perfect. The best way to deal with the inevitable talk about them was head-on. Arrive separately, walk into church together. A squeaky-clean new start.

No risking temptation. No causing additional gossip.

There'd be more than enough as it was.

Anna steered the van into the disabled parking space outside the building and it jerked to a halt. He shook his head. He wanted them riding around in an unsafe vehicle even less than he wanted them living in a house with a leaky roof.

Easy to guess what she'd answer if he offered to work on it for her. The same thing she'd say about him fixing her roof. A big fat no. He'd have to convince her.

Somehow.

Josh gave a wide grin and a wave. Anna's lips tightened in something nearer a grimace. She'd need time to accept the changes his arrival brought. And even more time to accept the truth about his past. He'd wait, until she knew the man he was now, thanks to God. Until she saw he wasn't going anywhere but here.

He hurried over, and opened the driver's door for her. Josh beamed from the back of the van.

At least one of them was happy to see him. The joy in his son's face constricted Luke's chest so tight he could hardly breathe.

Anna acknowledged him with a resigned not-quite-a-smile. "I should have known." She might not want him here, but with other churchgoers watching, they had no choice but to deal with the situation.

He grinned. "You know what they say, the family that prays together, stays together."

That earned him a roll of her lovely eyes. "We aren't a family."

He knew it. He couldn't force her to take the next step and accept his support. All he could do was knock, and wait for her to let him in. "No," he said. "But I am staying."

Anna didn't reply. She got out, moved to the back of the van, then strained to lift a metal ramp.

Luke stepped to her side. "Let me help." He put his Bible aside, took hold of the other ramp and easily slid it into place.

She shook her head, but surrendered the ramp she'd been battling with. "So brute force comes in handy now and then."

He just smiled, and secured the ramps.

"You're good to go, kiddo." She tapped the back of Josh's chair.

Josh's wheelchair motor whirred to life. Once he'd maneuvered down the ramps and out of the van, he twisted his neck to grin up at Luke. "I hoped you'd be here today."

Luke swallowed a boulder sized lump in his throat. "Let me help your mom, then we'll talk." He lifted the heavy ramps back into van.

Anna had struggled alone for too long.

"Will you sit with us in church?" Josh asked. "I want everyone to see that I've got a dad now, not just a mom." Like last night, he said mom like a swear word.

Anna bit her lip, and her shoulders tensed. The distress in her eyes pierced him. He understood Josh being angry, but it wasn't right Anna got blamed. He'd sit down with Josh sometime soon and explain things.

"Okay if I sit with you?" he asked her.

"Yes, of course." But her eyes held a warning — please don't mess up with everyone watching.

Eventually, she'd realize he truly was staying.

Maybe in another twelve years she'd trust him again?

He infused as much promise as he could into his smile, and spoke to Josh. "Lead the way, cowboy."

Josh powered up his wheelchair and they fell into step behind him on the narrow path.

Luke sneaked a sideways glance at Anna. Every time he saw her, she looked lovelier. If she'd grown a hard, untrusting shell, it didn't show in her soft and beautiful appearance. Her hair gleamed golden in the spring sunlight, and her skirt fluttered over the top of her boots as she walked. Her demure green sweater hinted at the sweet curves it hid, raising memories he'd better forget, fast.

Darkness beneath her eyes suggested she'd had a sleepless night. He longed to reach out and take her hand, comfort her, but he feared she'd pull away.

"Hello Uncle Roberto," Josh piped as they reached the arched white doors.

Luke dragged his gaze off Anna to smile at her neighbor, on greeter duty. The older man flicked him a twitch of his lips in response, loaded with suspicion.

"Guess what, Luke is my dad. Isn't that great?" Josh's wide grin as he grabbed Luke's arm left no one in any doubt of his feelings.

Their neighbor seemed less certain, but not surprised. Despite leaving the fundraiser before Josh's bombshell, he'd clearly heard the news. "I hope so, Josh," he said. "Maybe Miss Anna will let your father do some of the work round the house she hasn't permitted me to."

Anna stiffened. The older man smiled at her blandly, then threw Luke a glance that said "Help her, or else", as clear as if he spoke out loud.

"Mr Rodi, I hope she will too. I'm sorry I couldn't be completely honest with you when we met yesterday. Please forgive me for that." He laid a hand on Josh's shoulder, aiming to show his evasive answer had been for Josh's sake.

Roberto's tight lips relaxed a little, though his eyes still held warning.

Luke got the message. He'd be watched.

Other churchgoers queued behind them. Again, they had an audience. He'd better get used to that.

He reached for Anna's hand, and squeezed Josh's shoulder with his other hand. "Show me where we sit, cowboy."

Anna's hand quivered in his. He turned and smiled, wanting to reassure her. But something in their gazes held and sparked. His breath caught in his chest as the years they'd been apart disappeared. They were young again, in love, believing they could conquer any difficulty. Her wide startled eyes showed she felt it too.

For a moment, anything felt possible.

Then her lashes came down like curtains, and she snatched her hand free.

CHAPTER EIGHT

ANNA PULLED AWAY FROM LUKE and hurried down the aisle. She'd expected Luke would show up today, both to show he was serious about staying, and to kill any gossip by showing they had nothing to hide.

But she wasn't prepared for the way that when Luke took her hand, she felt seventeen again. Relived the old feelings that sent her straight into his arms, and straight into trouble.

Well, she wasn't seventeen any more.

She'd come home alone when Dad made her leave Eugene, and Luke. Walked back into church, pregnant and unmarried, burned by the shame and anger in Dad's eyes.

He'd taken her in again, sure. Some parents would have thrown her out. He'd even let her bring Josh home from the hospital. But the searing humiliation of publicly disgracing him, and the hurt of losing his love and approval would never leave her.

Pain twisted her heart. Just like then, she felt everyone's gaze on her.

She hesitated at their regular pew. No matter who went in first, she'd be seated next to Luke. Josh sat in an allocated space for his chair, at the end of a row.

"I want you to sit next to me," he said to Luke.

Josh still treated her like yesterday's trash. Knowing how much she'd upset him wrenched her. Sliding onto the old bench seat, worn smooth by a century of worship, she bowed her head, waiting for her usual calm to descend.

"Our church was built over a hundred and fifty years ago, in the Gold Rush. It's one of the oldest churches west of the Rockies." Josh proudly showed off his knowledge. "Nearly ten times as many people lived here, in tents and wooden shacks. That's why the church is bigger than we need now."

Luke smiled. "I'm glad one more worshiper today won't be a problem."

As he sat beside her, she made herself small, keeping distance between them so they didn't touch. Josh chattered happily to his father, relieving her of any need to speak. Taking slow deep breaths, she struggled to capture the elusive sense of peace she normally felt here.

She'd never known the deep relationship with God other believers seemed to have, but the simple holiness of the place usually fed something in her soul.

Not today. Not when Josh ignored her, Luke stirred emotions she didn't want to feel, and so many curious eyes watched them. She kept her head bowed and tried not to let it get to her. Once the service started, the congregation would have something else to think about besides her and Luke.

Dan preached on the damage wagging tongues could cause. It couldn't be more obvious he'd chosen the topic with them in mind. She snuck a sideways glance at Luke, steeling herself against the inevitable jolt in her chest. His calm profile gave nothing away.

As if he felt her gaze, he turned and smiled, but she looked away before their eyes connected. If Luke left them, the way she feared he would, Josh's heart would be broken. She couldn't chance her own heart.

But that didn't explain why she'd put on her prettiest skirt, and taken extra time over her hair. Why her heart had given that little bump at seeing him in the parking lot, or why her tummy fluttered with awareness of him. Staying strong for Josh meant resisting those responses.

In the thanksgiving prayers, Dan included Luke volunteering to lead the building team, with an impressive list of what he'd achieved in twelve years in the mission field. She couldn't quite figure that part out. Luke wasn't even a believer when they'd met.

Yet he'd grown into a man of faith, worthy of respect.

Her? She just didn't know. The lukewarm faith she'd grown up with gave little comfort. She'd never understand how God worked His plans. Josh's illness. Losing Mom and Dad. And now Luke.

Peering past him, carefully not letting her gaze linger on his broad chest or strong jaw, she checked on Josh. He sat as tall and straight as he could. Pride in his father blazed from him.

A quiet sigh escaped her. She didn't want to feel this hurt. Luke was Josh's dream come true, an answer to his prayers. She couldn't take that away from him. But she'd stay strong. Remembering the way Luke walked out of her hospital room clenched her soul. She couldn't go there again.

After the service came the real trial. Running the gauntlet of the gossips.

Tabby Whytecliff jockeyed into pole position with a smug grin. "Anna, fancy you keeping Luke hidden away in the mission field all these years. And he's volunteering here now. How wonderful. Is he making an honest woman of you at last?" Her saccharine tone hid barbs.

Once, Anna would have crumpled, too ashamed to stand up for herself. Now, she straightened her back and pinned on a smile. "I don't believe being a single mom makes me a dishonest woman, Mrs. Whytecliff."

Tabby opened her mouth, not doubt to fire off something more cutting.

For all her resolve not to need Luke, not to depend on him, Anna looked to him, praying he'd read the plea in her eyes. They had to play this right, for Josh's sake.

She needed his help.

No mistaking Anna's desperate glance. Luke made his excuses to Dan, and headed over. Her strained smile suggested Tabby had claws. He'd brave far more than the town gossips to earn the flash of gratitude in Anna's eyes.

"I was just telling Anna how wonderful it is that you've finally come back from your missionary work," Mrs. Whytecliff said. The emphasis on 'finally' gave her sweet words a nasty aftertaste. No wonder Anna wanted rescuing.

He took Anna's arm, and she trembled a little. "I'm grateful to have the opportunity to help Anna with Josh now, after my years serving God overseas."

Wheels almost whirred in Tabby's eyes as she looked from him to Anna, trying to work out their relationship. "You must give a talk to our ladies' group about your work."

"I'd love to." He'd talk all day about the charity. Anything to stop her upsetting Anna. "My priorities are spending time with Josh, and setting up the church building project. Once that's organized, we'll make a date." He gave her his best smile and a warm, two-handed handshake.

Flustered, she loosed an uncertain giggle. When he released her hand she bustled away to confer with a gaggle of other ladies.

Next came Maggie from the diner. No need to second guess her intentions. She pulled him into a hug, her smile wide and genuine. "I know you've never visited Sweetapple Falls before, but I'm glad you've come home." Her eyes twinkled with humor, kindness, and questions.

Josh tugged his arm. "Come on Luke. I want to show you our house."

Anna glanced at her watch and smiled apologetically at Maggie. "Gotta go. We'll catch up another time."

They rushed through the other introductions. He must have shaken fifty hands. Sensing Anna's need to get away, he didn't linger. Chat could wait for other Sundays.

The deputy didn't approach, eyeing them from across the church. Connor didn't like or trust him, that was obvious. Luke's sudden involvement in Anna's life wouldn't be welcome. He'd noticed the warmth in the lawman's eyes when they rested on her.

At last, he was alone with Anna in the parking lot, while Josh talked to a friend. "May I come to the house?" he asked. "We need to work things out."

"You've already promised Josh, so I can hardly refuse." Her pinned-on smile gave little clue how she felt.

Josh wheeled over to them. "I want to walk home. It's a nice day. We can pick up the van later." The disrespectful note in Josh's voice when he spoke to Anna made Luke uncomfortable. This strain between mother and son was his responsibility.

She raised her eyebrows. "You mean *I* can pick up the van later, don't you, kiddo?"

He'd bring the van back for her. See if it drove as badly as it looked and sounded. Anna and Josh using such a clunker bothered him.

As they set off along the quiet street, the fresh green of budding trees showed renewal and new life. He hoped that was true for them, as well.

"What did you do while you were away?" Josh asked. "Mrs. Whytecliff said you were a missionary, but Pastor Dan said you built houses."

Luke looked for signs of resentment, and saw none. The boy's face was open and interested. Only Anna bore Josh's bitterness.

"I wasn't exactly a missionary. I worked for a Christian charity, helping people build their own homes. We shared God with them too, of course, when we could."

"So you went to building school?"

Luke swallowed. He didn't want to damage his son's fragile trust in him, but Josh wasn't being fair to Anna, and that had to stop.

Staying around meant having the difficult conversations. Anna walked a little apart from them, primly gazing straight ahead, but Luke knew she was listening. Maybe she'd respect the man God made him into, and forget the loser he'd been.

Even if he didn't want her to know yet quite how much of a loser.

"No. I started as a laborer, doing grunt work. House the World taught me everything. Not only how to build a house, but who Jesus is, even how to read and write properly."

"You couldn't read or write? But everyone can!" Josh didn't look disgusted, just puzzled.

Luke shook his head, his lips twisted in a humorless smile. "Not everyone. Remember how you had to learn?"

Josh nodded.

"Your mom gave you a good home and sent you to school. But my mom and I moved around a lot and I never had much time in school. I could write a few words, but that was it."

Thankfully, Anna didn't ask more. He'd never spoken of his past when they were dating, and he didn't plan to now, either. Josh let it go, too.

There was telling the truth, and then there was too much

information. He hoped they never learned the whole truth about his past. Anna saw in black and white, the way Deputy Harrison taught her.

Some things, she'd never accept or understand.

Asking about the town kept the conversation on safer topics the rest of the way. Josh gladly showed off his knowledge of every building they passed. It didn't take long to reach Anna's big Victorian.

Luke's hands itched to restore it to its former glory. Patching the roof so Anna and Josh would stay dry for starters, then painting and repairing. Given time, he could make the old house shine again.

Anna unlatched it and waved him in, her lips softening in an almost-smile. Hope pulsed through him. Maybe she *would* allow him to work on the place.

Josh pushed his controls forward and shot through the gate ahead of them. "I'll check on Pattie."

"We always go this way," Anna explained. "I made the back yard wheelchair friendly and had a ramp put in for Josh at the back, but kept the porch steps at the front." Her eyes warmed, sweet and genuine. "That's how we know if a visitor is a stranger or a friend. Only strangers or bringers of bad news use the front door."

"So, am I a back door visitor now?" Luke kept his voice light, not wanting to show how much her answer meant.

She gave him a long measuring look, then her lips twisted ruefully. "I guess you're going to have to be."

Anna watched Luke and Josh through the mudroom window while she did the laundry. She wouldn't normally do it on Sunday, but she needed to do something.

She'd never felt closed out of Josh's life the way she did now. He'd ignored her the whole way home from church, focusing on Luke. Then when Luke returned from collecting the van, Josh dragged him out to the yard.

Boys only.

They had their heads close together, discussing something. Pattie Pork Pie lolled at Luke's feet, and he leaned down to scratch behind the pig's ear. He'd won over her son, her neighbors, even Pattie.

But definitely not her.

If she repeated it often enough, she might even convince herself.

She didn't know what to think of the man. He seemed to have turned his life around, with a faith that dwarfed hers. He showed determination and willingness to help with Josh. Her heart turned somersaults whenever she was within ten feet of him. But three days back in their lives meant nothing.

Except that things would never be the same.

Focusing on Josh's dirty clothes didn't stop her restless thoughts. He used to look at her with the same adoring gaze he now directed at Luke. Then this last year, he'd changed. He didn't want her doing so much for him.

Yet his disability made him as dependent as the average three year old. Balancing the need to let him go against her need to protect and care for him was a tightrope walk across Niagara Falls.

Juggling chainsaws.

Josh hadn't forgiven her for keeping Luke a secret. She needed to talk to him. Apologize. Ask his forgiveness. Help him see that even if she'd made the wrong choices, she'd wanted what was best for him.

She and Luke had been too young. But even though she wasn't strong enough to stand up to Dad, she'd truly loved Luke.

He had to stay this time. Not for her sake. For Josh. It was one thing to play at being a good time dad. Getting down and dirty in the reality of being a parent was something else. Luke had never done that. He was brand new, spotless, and a man.

No wonder Josh idolized Luke and blamed her.

He'd never been the one to discipline Josh. He'd never been the one to make Josh eat his vegetables. He'd never stood over Josh to make him do his homework when he wanted to play his new computer game. He'd never held Josh while he had labs drawn. He'd never cleaned out a stinky pigsty because Josh wanted a pet pig he couldn't care for.

A grin spread across her face. Maybe it was time he found out. Luke wanted to be part of Josh's life? Okay, let him prove it. If he was going to run away from the realities of fatherhood, better he did it now, rather than wait till Josh was even more attached to him.

She transferred a load of laundry from the washer to the dryer, picked up a towel, and wiped her hands. Luke was about to get a crash course in the realities of being a dad.

Her grin disappeared when she got outside and saw what they'd moved on to. Roberto had joined them in the drive. They poked at her van's engine, deep in discussion while Josh listened in. She didn't understand half what they said, but it sounded technical, it sounded expensive, and it sounded like they'd already decided what they were going to do.

Luke turned to her with a warm smile. She tightened her tummy to stop it doing a flip in response.

"If you'll let me, Roberto will lend me his tools and workshop to fix up the van."

Anna replied to Roberto, not Luke. "Roberto, I've told you before, it's fine. We can manage."

The older man shook his head. "Now you have a man in your life, he will take care of the things you wouldn't let me help you with. You cannot refuse to allow a father to keep his son safe."

She bristled. She didn't want Luke in her life, she was simply stuck with him.

Checking no one's hands were in the way, she slammed the van's hood. "I would never do anything to endanger Josh."

"The brakes and steering aren't safe," Luke said gently. "Driving the van every day, you wouldn't notice them gradually worsen. But if they're not repaired, you're risking an accident."

"Mom, you gotta let Luke and Uncle Roberto fix it. They'll teach me how everything works." Josh's mulish expression told her how he'd respond if she refused.

Since Luke's arrival, her sweet well-behaved son had catapulted into a sulky almost-teen. Once again, she couldn't say no.

Josh wanted his father involved in his life, and she couldn't deny him that.

If Luke broke his heart, they'd just have to deal with it.

But could she control her own unruly heart around Luke, when she'd have to see so much of him?

CHAPTER NINE

LUKE HELD HIS BREATH as he swept up pig berries, wishing he had a clothes pin for his nose. He'd been handed a broom and landed with cleaning duty the minute Roberto left.

Anna's attitude left him in no doubt she intended it as a test.

Was he here for the long haul, willing to do the dirty jobs that came with parenthood?

Josh watched from his chair while Pattie snuffled happily in the fresh straw Luke spread on the other side of her run. "I wish I could do that. She's my pig. I should be taking care of her."

Luke smiled at his son. "I don't mind, and I'm sure your mom never complains either."

"No. She doesn't complain." Josh's small voice hardened at the mention of Anna.

Luke stopped cleaning and moved to sit on an upturned box, next to the boy. Then he hesitated.

Being straight with Josh risked damaging their developing bond. But he'd glimpsed the hurt in Anna's eyes each time Josh spoke rudely to her, or turned to him rather than to her. If he could fix that, he would. "Seems you're upset with your mom."

Josh's expression turned sulky, his lower lip protruding. "She was going to let someone else adopt me. She didn't want me."

Luke shook his head. "She had tough decisions to make, and did what she thought was right. Your Gramps was a strong man and didn't give her much choice. But she loved you too much to let you go."

"But why didn't she tell you about me. Why didn't she want me to see you on Friday, and yesterday? She didn't want me to have my dad." His expression shifted, questioning rather than sullen.

Luke blew out a painful breath. "It's more my fault as hers. I wasn't a good person when you were born. I got angry and I went away. She had no way to contact me. So your mom wanted to wait, and be sure I wouldn't leave. That's what good moms do."

"You told me you were staying." Josh's brow furrowed and his voice wobbled, as his eyes begged for reassurance.

"I am. That's why I volunteered to fix the church, so I can stay." Luke poured all the certainty he could into his smile. "You need to be patient with your mom. This is a big change for us all."

Josh nodded slowly. "But I want her to like you. Then you could get married and live here, not at Pastor Dan's. I'd see you all the time."

Luke's chest warmed at the thought of him and Anna, married. Together as a family, sharing breakfast in that sunny yellow kitchen.

Crazy to hope for that.

He raised his hands. "Slow down cowboy! Your mom will need time to start to like me again. Liking me enough to get married? That may never happen. No matter what, I'll be nearby. I'll make sure I see you as much as I can." He took a deep breath, praying he wasn't pushing too hard. "Your anger with your mom is making it harder for her to accept me being here. Are you being fair to her?"

Josh looked down. One hand fiddled with the control of his chair, ready to retreat. So Josh inherited more than his blue eyes from his father. That tendency to run, too.

But this time, Luke wouldn't run when things got tough.

He waited. With the Mexican kids, he'd discovered sitting quietly would get them to open up if they were going to. Keeping his mouth shut, he stuck an encouraging smile on his face.

Finally Josh raised his eyes. "She didn't tell me about you. That's not fair either. I'm twelve. I should have been the one to decide if I wanted to meet you or not." He sounded oddly mature. Then he went back to kid again. "I'm not going to stop being mad at her, and you can't make me."

"I'm not going to try to make you. We all feel mad at times. It's staying mad that's the problem. Do you know that Bible verse, 'In your anger, do not sin'?"

Josh nodded uncertainly, as if not sure where this was leading.

He needed to make Josh understand, ease the kid's combative attitude to Anna. "None of us are perfect, we all make mistakes. People do things that upset us, but we need to forgive."

Vivid memories of his own mom, the last time he'd seen her, dragged him back into the past, into their apartment where she lay dead on the floor. Again, he was that angry, confused, hurting kid, not knowing what to do except run.

His stomach twisted. He couldn't quite forgive his mom for the choices she'd made. Not yet. Maybe, not ever.

Josh looked at him with a puzzled frown, his head tipped to one side like a sparrow.

Luke pinched his fingers over the lump where his nose had been broken the night his mom died, and dragged his focus into the present. This was about Josh and Anna, not him. "Your mom has always tried to do her best for you, hasn't she?"

Josh bit his lip, the same way Anna did, but gave a tiny nod.

"She meant the best for you with this, too." Luke sucked in a breath. "Would you ask God's help to forgive her? We could pray together right now if you want?"

The boy's face lit up like a floodlight had been switched on. "Can we? I'd like that. Me first."

"Sure thing, cowboy." The boy's enthusiasm awed Luke.

Josh reached out and took Luke's hand in his small one, and bowed his head. "Dear Jesus, thank You for giving me a dad, like I asked. And thank You that he wants to pray with me and he's interested in my stuff and Pattie likes him. So please would You keep him here with us so we can be a real family one day when Mom decides she likes him again. And I'm sorry I was mad at her. Please forgive me and I'll make it up to her. Amen."

Luke hadn't closed his eyes. He'd kept them open, watching his son. Thanksgiving swelled in his chest, warmer and sweeter than ever.

Josh squeezed his hand and grinned. "Your turn."

Luke bowed his head. "Lord, thank You for this blessing I never expected. My son is a boy any man would feel proud to call his son. Help me to be a father Josh can be proud of, too. Thank You, Lord

Jesus. Amen."

He whispered another prayer he didn't want Josh to hear. *Please, help me live up to the responsibility of being Josh's dad. I don't know how to be what I never had. I need You to show me how.*

He opened his eyes.

A tremulous smile hovered on Josh's lips. His thin hand shook in Luke's grasp. "Do you mean that? You really are proud of me?" The kid sounded so doubting, so unsure.

"Of course I mean it."

The biggest smile possible spread across Josh's face, bright as the sun, moon, and stars all rolled into one. "I'm glad you came to find me."

A matching goofy grin stretched Luke's face. "I'm glad I found you, too."

"I gotta go tell Mom I'm sorry. I should do it now, shouldn't I?" Josh jiggled his chair control, still grinning.

Luke nodded. "Good idea." He pushed himself to his feet and picked up his broom again. "I'll finish getting Miss Pattie's run cleaned out and come in once I'm done."

"Okay, Dad." Josh said the word tentatively at first, as if trying out the taste of it. "Dad," he said more firmly.

"Son." Luke reached out, taking Josh's frail body into a hug.

Thank You, thank You, thank You chorused in his heart, loud enough for heaven to dance to the tune. God couldn't give him any greater gift in this moment than Josh calling him Dad.

Apart from perhaps someday, Anna welcoming him back into their lives.

Anna couldn't stop herself peeking out the window at Josh and Luke.

She tried to tell herself she wasn't watching them together. The laundry sorting table was right in front of the window. Of course she'd look up from time to time as she paired socks and folded shirts. She was looking at the garden, not them. Grandmother's old lilac was starting to bud. Spring blossom would soon be on the fruit trees.

But she knew it wasn't the garden her attention clung to.

Normally, she loved this season for its newness, its hope and possibilities. But things didn't feel too hopeful right now. She could see her son slipping away from her, right in front of her eyes, as Luke and Josh hugged.

Josh looked pitifully frail, thin arms struggling to reach Luke's broad back.

He looked up, staring straight at the window. She turned away, vision blurring as tears stung her eyes. What was wrong with her? She never cried. Yet since Luke's return, it seemed that was all she did.

He came back into her life, and everything changed.

Josh knew the truth. And for better or for worse, she was stuck with Luke.

The back door opened and Josh's chair whirred. She swiped at her eyes, pasted a good mom smile on her face, and walked into the kitchen. Josh sat at the open refrigerator, drinking juice straight from the carton. She ought to tell him off, like she usually would, but she couldn't bear making things even worse between them.

He put the carton back quickly, shut the fridge door, and turned his chair toward her. "Sorry, Mom. I'll use a glass next time, promise."

Her stomach clenched as she saw his tear-streaked face. "Josh, what's wrong?"

He grinned. "Nothing's wrong. Luke is awesome. We even prayed together. Him coming home is the best thing that's happened to me, ever. Even better than Talent Trek."

She should be glad for her son. But she couldn't feel it. All she felt was hurt. Dragging in a breath, she chose her words carefully. "I'm pleased you're happy. It's a big thing having your father come back into our lives like this."

She paused. Though it burned in her throat to do it, she had to apologize. Nothing would convince her she'd been wrong in wanting to wait until Luke proved he was staying.

Nothing but the memory of Josh's pain last night.

"I'm sorry —"

Both of them said the same words at once, then stopped. They looked at each other and laughed. A forced tinny laugh, sure, but the first they'd shared since last night.

"You go first," she said.

"No, you go first, Mom."

She filled her lungs slowly, and let the air go. "Okay. I want to apologize for not telling you sooner about your dad." She ducked her head, then forced herself to meet his eyes. This was harder than she expected. "I thought it was the right thing to do, but I was wrong."

Some of the tension in Josh's face relaxed.

Her own tight shoulders dropped as relief filled her. Hopefully, her fears about Luke leaving were wrong, too. "I'm sorry I didn't tell you the truth on Friday when he first arrived, or on Saturday afternoon."

"That's so funny. I came in to tell you I was sorry for being mad at you about it. Luke said I needed to forgive you. We prayed about it and I knew he was right. You didn't do it on purpose to keep him a secret and keep me a kid. And you didn't want to have me adopted, Gramps made you. So I'm sorry I was mean to you. I'm not angry now."

Josh's bright smile felt like sunrise in her heart. Maybe she hadn't lost him as much as she'd feared. And Luke had supported her with Josh. That meant something.

A big something.

"I'm glad. I didn't like you being angry with me. Truce?"

She desperately wanted to hug him the way Luke had, but something told her to offer a hand for him to shake, as if he was an adult. Something had changed in their relationship, forever.

But he was still her son. Still her responsibility. Still the center of her heart.

That's how it would always be, no matter what happened with Luke.

As if he knew she'd thought of him, Luke knocked on the open back door and poked his head around it. She managed a smile.

"Pig detail completed, ma'am." His smart salute complete with wobble made Josh giggle.

Her own tight smile relaxed, felt more natural on her face.

Luke lifted his hands and spoke in his normal voice. "Where can I clean up?"

She pointed him to the sink in the mudroom, and watched, mesmerised, as he lathered and rinsed his strong hands and tanned forearms. Picking up a towel to pass to him, she stepped forward, just as he turned. They bumped together, knocking her off balance, and he grabbed her arm to support her. His wet hand burned through her thin sweater.

Their gazes connected, and her breath caught as memories

flooded her. The way he'd held her when they were in love. The way he'd promised to love her forever.

Thrusting the towel at him, she jumped back, keeping her distance, careful not to touch him again. Being around Luke was dangerous. Her emotions were too susceptible to him. She had no intention of risking her heart again. They'd be Josh's Dad and Mom, no more.

Yet after just a few days, it already felt more.

Anna struggled to focus on painting the old picket fence at the front of the house. But when she slopped white paint onto the ground instead of the fence for the third time, she had to admit it. Her mind wasn't on the job.

Luke was such a distraction. Working alongside him proved harder than she'd expected.

When he'd arrived on Monday morning offering to fix up her house, an instinctive refusal rose to her lips. But he'd claimed they needed to use this fine sunny weather while it lasted. And that it would give him something useful to do while he waited for material and equipment he needed for the church work to arrive.

Josh fizzed with excitement at the chance of some father-son time over Spring Break, and was quick to figure that if Luke fixed the roof for them, he could have that skiing trip he wanted, after all.

She'd bitten back her no, for Josh's sake. Having the cash to take him now was a blessing she couldn't refuse. He might not be well enough next winter.

Three days later, Luke had them all busy working. He'd been at the house long hours every day, working harder and doing better work on the house than any paid contractor would have done. He had the roof watertight in two days, and then moved on to repairing, sanding, nailing, and painting, with Josh anxious to help.

So instead of painting landscapes in her studio, she painted the fence instead, unable to stop herself listening and watching as Luke showed Josh how to hammer loose fence palings back into place.

Anxiety for Josh flooded her at first. Then she'd seen how carefully Luke chose jobs Josh could handle and how closely he watched over the boy. He'd even found a lightweight hammer for

Josh. His care for their son warmed her.

Helping Josh get a grip on the hammer, he slid it further back in Josh's hand. "Hold it like this, nearer the end of the handle. Too close to the head means you lose a lot of the force when you hit. That's called choking the hammer."

She tried to ignore the way his arm and shoulder muscles flexed beneath his T-shirt as he bent over Josh, demonstrating with his own full size hammer how to hit the nail.

She tried to ignore the way the deep honeyed timbre of his voice melted something in her, as he pulled out a crooked nail and explained lever action to Josh.

She tried to ignore the memory of his strong hands holding her, as he showed Josh how to fit the new nail into the paling first, so he'd have one hand free to hold it while he hammered.

For all she told herself she was only keeping an eye on her son, and Luke didn't affect her one bit, she couldn't deny he stirred her emotions as much now as he had at eighteen.

More so, seeing his kindness and patience with Josh's clumsy movements. He'd shown maturity, strength, and faith, in everything he'd done since coming here. Thankfully, he couldn't guess how dry her mouth was, or how her heart fluttered.

Maybe it wasn't Luke who did that to her. The warm day. The paint fumes. Needing lunch.

Had to be.

But she knew she was kidding herself.

"Keep going, you're nearly there," he encouraged Josh.

A few more unsteady bangs of the hammer, and Josh shouted out. "I did it! Mom, look, I hammered a nail! Now this paling won't fall down." He turned to her, face jubilant.

Her heart clenched and her teeth clamped on her lip to stop from crying. She bent down, hiding her face, more careful than she needed to be resting her paintbrush across the top of the tin. Josh mustn't see how much his joy in doing such a simple task moved her.

A couple of deep breaths, and she had herself under control. As she lifted her head, her eyes met Luke's. The understanding she saw in his gaze jolted her to the core.

He knew how she felt. He felt it too. They shared things no one else could fully understand or appreciate. Rather than scaring her, the thought comforted her.

"He's a natural. I couldn't have done it better." Luke reached out and gave her arm a squeeze as he spoke.

His touch sent a surge of warmth along her skin. The sensible thing would be to step back, pull her arm away, resist the betraying heat flooding all the way down to her trembling toes. But she didn't.

Instead, she stepped nearer. Running a finger over the top of the nail Josh had driven home, she admired his work, and forced her voice to stay calm and steady, as if Luke's touch didn't have her breathless as a marathon runner.

"Great job, Josh. I can't drive a nail straight to save my life. You clearly inherited that from your dad."

Luke and Josh both looked fit to burst with pride. They grinned at each other, then at her. Those matching high-voltage grins gave her heart such a jolt she put a hand to her chest to check it kept beating.

So soon, they'd started to feel like a family. How could that be possible?

CHAPTER TEN

"I NEED TO START MAKING LUNCH." Unnerved by Luke's closeness, Anna rushed into an excuse and hurried indoors.

She'd seen enough of how he worked to know he'd take good care of Josh. She didn't need to hover, ready to helicopter in at the first sign of trouble. In the kitchen, safely away from his disturbing presence, she leaned on the counter and took a few deep calming breaths.

Or they were supposed to be calming.

Now she was at a safe distance and couldn't see him, she should be able to get her focus back. Instead, hearing more hammering and his deep voice as he chatted to Josh, all her awareness still centered on him.

This wasn't how it was supposed to be.

She should be strong, cool, able to deal with this. Just Josh's parents, nothing more.

But the words she kept repeating to herself didn't seem to work.

Lord, I don't know what to do about the way I feel for Luke. I can't do this on my own anymore. I need Your help.

She didn't feel God heard her, but maybe the prayer did bring a little calm to her spirit. She busied herself with meal preparation, slapping some burgers under the grill, washing salad leaves, cutting up tomatoes, singing an old favorite hymn as she did. "Count your blessings, name them one by one, count your blessings, see what God has done…"

Then Luke opened the back door. She jumped, and the knife

slipped in her hand, slicing into her finger.

"Ouch!" Blood oozed from a shallow cut. Nothing serious, but tears still stung her eyes at the sudden pain.

Luke hurried to her side and wrapped a supporting arm around her, leading her to the sink. He turned on the tap, and held her hand under it. "Let the water wash it clean."

Was it the surprise of the cut or Luke's closeness making her weak? Such a small wound shouldn't leave her trembling, and needing to lean against him the way she did.

Gathering her strength, she straightened and pulled away from him. "I'm fine. I'll just wrap it in a square of kitchen towel."

Luke eyed her as she flopped in one of the straight-backed wooden chairs and handed her a clean sheet or towel. "I'll call Josh in and take over the lunch prep for you."

"I'm fine. It's only a scratch. See, it's stopped bleeding." She lifted the paper towel she'd pressed to the small wound and held up the finger.

It had stopped bleeding, but her protest sounded weak even to her own ears. How could she tell him his presence was the problem, affecting her far more than the minor injury?

"I'm happy to cook. I did KP often enough on our housing projects." He turned to the grill and expertly flipped the burgers. "Would you tell me where I can find some plastic wrap? That's what I came in for. I want to wrap your paintbrush, so the paint doesn't set hard."

She stood and pulled a roll from a drawer. Their fingers brushed as she handed it to him, and her breath caught. Then he moved toward the door, and she could breathe again.

"I'll fix the painting gear up, then get Josh in. We can both help with lunch." His cheerful smile gave no indication the simple touch affected him the way it had her.

Luke was every bit the man she'd dreamed of at seventeen, and more.

Dad's disapproval and anger still echoed in her mind. The memory of seeing Luke walk from her hospital room still shattered her. All the losses she'd known told her not to let him into her heart again.

But he was back in her life, and she had no idea what to do about the emotions he stirred in her.

Luke smiled at Josh as the kid passed a spanner to him.

Having to wait till Saturday to start on the church building gave him the perfect excuse to work on Anna's house and van. The delays getting lumber ripped and scaffolding delivered became unexpected blessings.

Josh being off school on Spring Break and Anna allowing them so much time together were even bigger blessings. He'd been here working most of every day this week, going back to Dan's when the sun set.

The only catch was the way Anna avoided him, in an almost comical dance.

But he was here for Josh, not Anna. The kid loved doing what he called "man stuff", and took to it like a natural, quickly grasping the theory behind whatever they worked on. Today he'd deserted painting for the chance to help tinker with the van.

Luke bent over the engine, tightening loose bolts. That should stop a few of the vehicle's many rattles. "We'll have it running like a dream by the time we've finished, partner."

"As long as it's not a nightmare." Josh grinned back. "It's great that we can do this. My friends all help their dads." He felt silent. "I asked Roberto, but he said no. Mom told him not to let me help. But I want to. It's fun."

Luke followed Josh's gaze across the yard to Anna, rhythmically spreading lemon yellow paint along the clapboards. The color suited her. Sunshine, happiness, Anna — they went together. Her golden hair glinted as her pony tail swung from side to side with her movements.

He shouldn't be noticing how her paint-spattered T-shirt and faded jeans clung to her full curves. She'd made it clear he was here as Josh's dad, nothing more. He got time with Josh, but time with her was a definite no-go.

Though he'd glimpsed flashes of warmth in her eyes. Those brief moments raised his spirits and gave him hope she'd reconsider, given patience and time.

Dragging his gaze away from her, he turned back to Josh. "Your mom wants to know you're safe."

"She worries too much. She won't let me do things much younger kids do." Was Josh complaining about Anna, or the restrictions his illness put on him?

"Not being able to do what you want must be frustrating." Not that Luke knew how having someone care so much felt, but he tried to imagine. "You're blessed to have a mom who cares about you like she does."

Josh crinkled up his nose, then shrugged. "I guess I am blessed. She let me work with you. She let me do *Talent Trek*. We're going skiing." He stopped, looking at Luke. "Did your mom look after you the same?"

Luke bowed his head, wanting to give the right answer. At Josh's age, he'd never known moms like Anna existed outside of TV commercials. He sucked in a deep breath and rubbed the bridge of his nose, pushing down the tide of regret rising in him. "My mom wasn't well enough to take care of me."

No need to say more than that. Some realities of life Josh didn't need to know yet.

Besides, Anna could hear every word they said. He glanced toward her. Something in the lines of her body, a tension that hadn't been there before, told him she'd overheard.

He waited for the usual wave of shame at the thought of Mom to hit, but it didn't. Maybe God was healing those memories at last. Still, he chose his words carefully. "I had to spend some time living away from her, when she was really ill. Then she died when I was fifteen."

Josh shook his head. "I call her Smother Mother sometimes, but I'd hate it if my mom wasn't around." He was quiet for a moment. "Didn't you have a dad either? I was the only kid in my class who didn't."

Guilt expanded in Luke's chest, hot and painful. As much as he told himself it wasn't his fault, it still felt as if it was. "I'm sorry you went so long without a father. But I'm here now, and I'm staying."

He glanced at Anna as he spoke. She'd turned around, not making any pretense she wasn't listening.

Her eyes pleaded with him wordlessly, saying "You'd better."

"If you need me, I'll be here." His gaze connected with hers, making it clear the words were as much for her as Josh.

"But what about *your* dad," Josh persisted.

He threw Josh a twisted smile and bent over the engine again.

"You're one up on me, cowboy. I never met my dad."

Josh marked a point in the air with one finger, but his face kept its puzzled expression. Like Pattie Pork Pie when food was around, Josh didn't give up easy when he latched onto something. "Didn't you try to find him? I would have done, when I was old enough."

Luke shook his head. He'd been too busy surviving to search out family who obviously didn't want him. "I didn't get the chance. Though I've wondered about him, and my mom's parents too."

Josh's eyes widened. "You didn't meet them either? Why not? I can just remember Gramps and Nana."

Luke didn't want to mess up and say the wrong thing. He had no idea what Josh knew about the facts of life. He'd need to check that with Anna, and soon. "They didn't want anything to do with my mom, when she told them she was having a baby but wasn't marrying my dad. So it was her and me, on our own."

Josh looked thoughtful. "Like Mom and me after Gramps and Nana died."

He forced a smile. "Kind of like that, yes."

Luke peeked at Anna again. She'd turned back to the wall, though there wasn't much more paint on it than last time he'd looked. He wasn't going to tell Josh how bad things had been, or Anna either. She needed to trust him a lot more before she could hear the truth, and Josh was way too young.

But Josh wasn't finished yet. "So, now Mom likes you again, when are you two going to get married? She told me, that first night you came to our house, that if I found the man I wanted for my dad, she'd marry him. I want *you*. You already *are* my dad."

Luke stood up so fast he whacked his head on the van's raised hood. The bump had to be what made his heart beat faster. But as he rubbed the spot, longing swamped him.

Truth was, he'd like nothing better.

They'd proved this week they could work as a team. Anna seemed more accepting with every day. But now, back rigid and head turned, she slapped paint onto the wall as if her life depended on getting it done in record time. Her reaction doused his overheated hopes with ice water.

He forced a laugh. "I don't think your mom likes me that much yet, Josh. It takes a special kind of like to make a marriage work. And I've only been here a week. Some people know each other for years before they get married."

Josh opened his mouth to argue, but Luke got in first. Way past time to change the subject, before the kid asked anything else. "We need to get underneath the van to check the muffler system and brakes. I could lift you onto the slide board to come underneath too, if you want?"

Thankfully, that distracted Josh. For now, anyway.

Luke bent to pick up the spanner he'd dropped. Blame his red face on that, not his foolish hopes that what Josh asked for might really happen.

Convincing Anna to let him be more than Josh's dad was a long term project. Rebuilding trust couldn't be rushed. Skimp on the foundations, and the whole house would come tumbling down.

They'd gone wrong that way in the past. He didn't intend to make the same mistake again.

This time, what they built would be for keeps.

For the first time, Anna wasn't part of Josh's Friday movie and pizza night. Instead, he'd asked Luke to stay with him and his friends.

She'd smiled, said it was a good chance to catch up on her studio time. But she couldn't focus, and her expensive oil paints hardened on her palette. The quiet instrumental music she listened to couldn't compete with the sound of laughter drifting up the stairs.

She put the palette down and pressed her palms over stinging eyes.

This past week, Luke had been amazing. Josh was happier than she'd ever seen him. But Luke's presence pushed Josh over some invisible dividing line. He'd become a man-cub, wanting Dad, not Mom. Since Luke came back, everything turned upside down and inside out, and things would never be the same.

The past twelve years, she'd been wrapped up in caring for Josh. She tried to remember the last time she'd gone somewhere that didn't involve him, an adults-not-kids social event, and came up blank.

Every mom came to this point, she guessed. But she hadn't realized it would happen so soon.

Not with Josh.

This morning, they'd been running late with their routine, and

Luke arrived before they finished. Josh asked her to show Luke how to help with the stretches he hated. Josh actually laughed while he did them.

Now he wanted Luke to do the sessions every day, morning and evening.

Jealousy cut like a dagger she'd turned on herself. Bit by bit, she felt closed out of her son's life. She sank into her grandmother's old wicker chair and cupped her cooling mug of vanilla chai in her hands.

Josh had been the center of her life since the moment the nurse put him into her arms, still messy from birth, and instead of crying he'd looked up at her with serious indigo eyes. Letting him go ripped a gaping hole in her heart. Her fingers clenched on the mug.

She hadn't been able to let him go when he was a baby, and she wanted to cling to him now, too.

Yet she had to let him grow up. And she had to adjust to Luke being back in her life.

Like wool a kitten played with, her feelings tangled.

Grief at the inevitability of losing Josh as his illness progressed. Joy he had the father he wanted. Her old heartache over Luke disappearing. Respect for the man Luke had become.

And then there was that effervescent fizz tingling her nerves and hitching her breath and bubbling right through her when their eyes met and he smiled that sweet warm smile of his.

Footsteps sounded on the stairs and she looked up. Luke hesitated in the doorway, as if unsure he'd be welcome.

She put her mug on the low table beside her and jumped to her feet. Her heart did a funny little hiccup at the sight of him. So unfair, when she wanted to resist him. The curve of his lips, the way his tanned skin crinkled around the deep Prussian blue of his eyes, the way he looked at her as if he understood, recognized how hard all this was for her — all these only made it harder to bear.

She wanted to blame Luke for the tangle her life had become, though in her heart she knew trying to keep Josh a child wouldn't add any years to his life.

Luke and the risk he might leave them again just made a convenient target for her grief and her anger.

"I brought you some ice cream," he said, holding out a bowl. "But I don't want to interrupt your work."

Lips twisting, she waved at her chair and tea cup. "You can see how hard I was working. It's okay, come in."

He walked over to the unfinished canvas. "You're good. I never guessed how good." He turned from the painting toward her, dangerously close. "I wanted to buy a painting, that day in the cafe. I didn't know it was yours. I only knew I liked it."

Her heart unfurled like apple blossom in the warmth of his approval. "Thank you."

She didn't know what else to say. Everything about Luke sent her pulses pounding and her nerves twanging. His nearness. His heady male odor of soap and sweat piercing through the linseed oil and turpentine of her studio. His broad shoulders, inviting her to let him share the load.

"I'd better get back to the boys. But I didn't want you to miss out." As he bent to put the ice cream on the table, that wayward lock of hair of his drooped forward. Her fingers itched to push it back. Would it feel as springy and thick beneath her fingers as it used to?

She clenched her fists to stop herself touching to find out. She mustn't think such thoughts. Dared not think such thoughts. He mustn't guess how he affected her.

Those thoughts and feelings clouded her judgment too much.

He straightened, and stood looking at her. So close they were almost touching.

Something in his gaze made the breath catch in her throat. As if a magnetic force pulled her, she leaned nearer, lifting her face toward his until she felt his breath soft and warm on her face.

His intent eyes asked a question.

He must have seen the answer he sought, because his head dipped lower, slowly, so slowly, so she could step back any time she wanted. Except she didn't.

His lips found hers. Every bit as good as she remembered, firm and warm and sweet, tasting of ice cream. She melted into his kiss.

Then he pulled away, far too soon. Loss reverberated through her. She swayed where she stood. Luke cradled her face in both his hands. Tenderly. As if she was the most precious thing in world.

His strong hands trembled against her skin. Emotion flecked his storm dark eyes. "I don't want to rush you, Anna." His voice wasn't much above a whisper. "But thank you for letting me back into your life. And Josh's."

His lips brushed hers again, the lightest, feather-touch of a kiss that still sent tremors through her. She clamped down hard on her feelings, forced herself not to respond the way she yearned to.

Luke stepped away. "I mustn't leave the boys too long." Hoarseness roughened his voice. He hurried into the hall and down the stairs.

She stood, staring after him. His return made life so much more complicated.

Especially if she let herself fall in love with him again.

CHAPTER ELEVEN

ANNA GAVE THANKS THAT Luke went downstairs without trying to kiss her again last night, then left soon after the other parents picked up their sons. Probably the kiss surprised him as much as it did her.

She certainly didn't intend to let it happen again. The way her lips still tingled at the memory only reinforced that resolve.

Today, though of course he was also at the church working party, she'd managed to avoid him. Raising scaffolding and getting a temporary roof covering in place over the church kept half the work crew busy. The other half minded kids and prepared food and drink, ready for when the building work stopped.

She should be spreading butter on a hundred slices of bread for Maggie to make into sandwiches, but the trestle tables they worked on gave a ringside view of the building. Buttering bread didn't stop her attention straying to Luke.

He was hard to ignore.

Staff from the scaffolding company gave their instructions, but no one could doubt Luke was in charge as he moved around the site, assisting, advising, encouraging. He'd taken off his plaid flannel shirt and wore a short sleeved T-shirt, faded and shrunken from too many washes, and a hip-hugging tool belt over his jeans. His shoulders stretched the shirt. Even from here, the movement of the muscles in his forearms mesmerized her.

Strong arms that could support her and Josh. Broad shoulders a far too susceptible part of herself longed to cast her burdens onto.

And it seemed he'd grown a strong character to match. Become a man of faith, the sort of man a woman could depend on.

But could she take the risk of trusting again? Since Mom and Dad died, her focus had been on independence, needing no one.

Not even God, and especially not a man.

A spoon waved in front of Anna's face. She jumped, and turned to face Maggie.

The older woman's grin was all-too-knowing. "Come on girl! Plenty more sandwiches to make. I can't add mayo and fillings if the bread isn't buttered first." She tapped the spoon on her half-empty mayo bottle.

"Sorry! I was miles away." Anna betrayed herself by peeking at Luke again.

Maggie laughed. "A little nearer than a mile, I reckon. No wonder your Josh is so cute. His Daddy is a fine looking man."

Anna's cheeks heated. She picked up the knife and began spreading butter, fast as she could. "I was just checking Josh was okay." Her attempt at dignity wouldn't fool Maggie.

But it was true. Almost.

Checking Josh meant seeing Luke, too. Josh trailed behind his father like a puppy, surely slowing his progress, but Luke gave no hint of impatience. As he leaned down with a smile to explain something to Josh, no one seeing them together would guess he hadn't been there every day of his son's life.

"Such a blessing, God giving you two this second chance." Maggie's sunny smile didn't quite hide her longing to know the truth.

Anna focused on the bread, hoping the heat in her cheeks wasn't a betraying blush. "A second chance for Josh and his father, not for Luke and me."

Her voice sounded strong, even if she didn't quite convince herself. Part of her longed to open her heart and see where this unexpected reunion took them. Part of her wanted to lock her heart up tighter than ever.

Look what happened when she trusted people, depended on them? They died, or they left her.

Josh adored Luke. And if Luke left, he'd be devastated. She'd need to be strong enough to help Josh pick up the pieces of his shattered dreams.

Last night had been a mistake. Keeping Luke at arm's length was wise, sensible, prudent, all the things she needed to be, for Josh's sake. Yet her heart dropped to her sneakers at the thought.

Maggie looked around like a conspirator, checking Tabby and her group circulating with the home-made lemonade were out of hearing range. She reached out and stilled Anna's suddenly busy hand.

Anna tensed. Maggie had far kinder intentions, but gossiped just as much as Tabby.

"So, while no one else is around, tell me the truth. How's it working out?"

Anna didn't try to pretend not to understand. "Fine, just fine," she said slowly.

Maggie threw her an eyebrow-raised glance. "Really?"

Anna screwed her eyes tight shut before answering. How much dared she say? She did need to talk heart to heart with another woman. Not about Luke, as much as Josh. If Mom were still alive she could have talked about it with her, but Mom was gone, and Maggie was the closest thing to both a mom and a friend she had.

"Josh is happy, that's what counts. Luke is doing so much for him." She put the knife down and turned to Maggie. "I never realized how much Josh wanted his father. He thanks God every night for Luke."

"That's good, isn't it?" Maggie asked, brow crinkled.

Anna sighed and looked toward Josh, carefully making sure her gaze didn't linger on Luke. "Being Josh's mom has been the biggest part of my life for so long." She turned back to the older woman. "I'm jealous of the way he wants to spend all his time with Luke now. Yet a little relieved too, that Luke is helping so much. Okay, a lot relieved. You raised three kids, so tell me. Does that make me a bad mother?"

"That makes you normal. I don't know a Mom who wouldn't feel the same." Maggie laughed, loud and rich, comforting as hot chocolate.

Her understanding acceptance lifted a weight of guilt from Anna.

"It's not you and Josh I most want to know about." Maggie grinned, and shook her head. "It's you and Luke. You know that's what I meant, girl."

Anna did know that. She turned back to the bread, and buttered as fast as she could, pushing the slices toward Maggie. How could she explain that her feelings about Luke were even more of a mess than her feelings about Josh growing up?

"It's complicated. I can't make enough sense of how I feel to begin to tell you." Hoping to prevent any further questions, she tried to change the subject. "They'll be stopping for a break soon. We really need to get these sandwiches finished."

The older woman added fillings, slapped the sandwiches closed, and cut them neatly. Anna couldn't keep up with her pace.

"You don't wriggle away that easy. One thing you learn quick in a diner is how to work and talk at the same time." Maggie's chuckle shook her. "You know, honey, everything worthwhile in life is complicated. Your Luke is doing a good job out there. He's a natural born leader. The other men respect him."

"He's not my Luke," Anna protested.

But a treacherous part of her wished he really was her Luke. Maggie was right. He was doing a good job. With Josh, their house, and now with the church building work.

And also with her.

Josh's chair whirred behind them, and footsteps crunched the gravel. Luke. Had to be. That instant stir of awareness only happened with him.

"Could I grab a couple of sandwiches, please? I have a hungry assistant here." His warm voice made her stomach flip, but she didn't turn until he put his hand on her shoulder, firm and strong.

She knew she should step away.

She didn't. The smile in his dark eyes stopped her.

Could it be God wanted her to trust Luke again and give him another chance?

She couldn't. She just couldn't. The risk was too big. She'd been hurt too many times.

But part of her wanted to trust him, so badly.

Luke sat beside Josh at the potluck that evening, balancing a plate on his lap as the kid chattered about his plans for the ski trip.

"Noah will be there, and Alex, and George. Cade's mom said he might be able to come, too. It will be awesome." Enthusiasm and anticipation lifted his voice.

"Do you want to go talk to them now?" Luke gestured to the

noisy cluster of boys across the room.

"Nah. I want to stay with you." Josh's smile held such pride and warmth.

Joy swelled Luke's heart. He'd expected Josh would want to spend time with his friends, but the kid stuck by his side all day.

Not that he minded. Josh's this-is-my-Dad possessiveness was too precious to ignore.

As people passed, they nodded, smiled, or said a friendly word. Luke felt a welcomed part of the community. Even the deputy acted polite enough to his face, though his watchful gray eyes held a constant warning.

If he chose to dig, he'd easily find the dirt in Luke's past. The arrest and court records would be on file in Eugene.

Would the townfolk's welcome change if they knew?

Luke just prayed that if Connor did go digging, Anna would know the man he was now well enough to trust and forgive him.

He'd been a fool to kiss her last night.

When she looked up at him with something irresistible shining in her eyes, the love for her he'd never lost welled up in him. But though he'd backed off fast instead of deepening the kiss as he'd longed to, her avoidance tactics today were unmistakable.

He hoped that kiss wouldn't wreck his chances of being there when Josh first skied. His best memory of his childhood was the winter he turned ten. Mom stayed off the drugs long enough to get a job in a ski lodge, and they'd spent all their spare time skiing.

That winter, he'd felt he really had a mom.

Once he found the right moment, he'd ask Anna if he could tag along. With a group of parents and kids, if he got his own room, it wouldn't cause gossip.

"Do you know anything about girls?" Josh asked suddenly.

Luke stared at Josh, and set his plate to one side before he dropped it. He was the last guy to ask.

Anna had been his only girlfriend, and he'd messed up badly there. At Josh's age, he'd been more worried about where his next meal was coming from. He fingered his crooked nose, broken trying to stop Mom's boyfriend beating her. After that night, he'd lived on the streets.

His teens had been anything but normal.

"Not much." He shrugged. "Not many girls on construction

sites."

"But you must have had a girlfriend sometime?" Josh persisted.

Luke looked over to Anna, emerging from the kitchen with a bowl in each hand. Just a glance, but her eyes met his for an instant. Then she looked away so fast it was obvious — she'd decided the cold shoulder was the way to go.

He'd blown it with that kiss.

Swiveling back to Josh, he forced a smile. "Your mom and I dated, sure. But that was a long time ago."

Josh nodded. He took a deep breath, squeezed his eyes shut, and bit his lip before speaking. "So, can I ask you a question?" He raised one bent hand and rubbed it over his mouth. "Mom said for advice on boy stuff I should talk to Pastor Dan or Deputy Connor. But I can't talk to the Pastor about girls, and I can't talk to the Deputy about this." He gazed across the room.

Luke followed his stare to where Connor stood protectively beside a pretty red haired girl wearing glasses. "Is that his daughter?"

Josh turned back to Luke, eyes big and expression dreamy. He nodded. "Lisa. She's in my class."

Uh oh. Looked like the kid had his first crush, and had it bad. Did Anna know? "I see why talking to the Deputy might not help. Ask away, cowboy. I'll do my best to answer."

Josh looked suddenly serious. "How do I know if a girl likes me? And how do I ask her on a date?" He looked down at himself and his face twisted. "I know I'm only twelve and I'm in this chair and the doctors say I'll die before I'm thirty if I even make it out my teens. But I like her."

Luke swallowed hard, but the lump in his throat didn't budge. Josh's tone was so matter of fact, so accepting. The kid's resigned smile cracked something in Luke's chest wide open.

Josh's teens would be anything but normal, too.

Please Lord, give him time. To date, and do so much else. And help me give him an answer. Fielding dating questions wasn't on my parenting radar.

Somehow, he managed to reply. "I think the deputy would say she's too young to date yet. Maybe do things in a group, like going to lunch or seeing a movie?"

"We already do that. But I get tongue-tied with her." Josh laughed and rolled his eyes. "I know, I'm usually Mr. Talk."

Luke glanced back to Lisa. Connor had moved away, and his

daughter peered toward Josh, giggling with another girl. She must have realized he'd noticed, because she looked away and blushed.

Stifling a smile, he wondered if Lisa was doing almost the same as Josh right now — asking her friend whether she thought Josh liked her.

He turned back to Josh.

"That's normal with a girl you like. Just be her friend. Help her with her homework or teach her chess or do something else she might be interested in." He smiled. "And if you can't talk to her, listen. One thing I do know about girls is that they like to be listened to."

"But how can I know if she likes me?" Josh persisted.

Luke laughed. "Wish I knew! But maybe, if she always seems to be where you are. If you catch her looking at you then looking away when you notice. If she listens to you, and seems interested. But if she really likes you, she'll make sure you know."

Josh nodded slowly, his gaze on Lisa and his expression thoughtful.

Luke remembered how Anna clung to him when he took her home on the back of his motorbike, the night they met. How she kept him talking at the entrance to her dorm, long after he should have left. How he'd somehow known she wanted to see him again.

Him, worthless messed-up him.

He'd felt like a king when she looked at him that way.

He glanced to the kitchen, and his stomach flipped over as their eyes met again. She immediately turned away.

One sign out of three. It was a start.

He'd keep on being Josh's dad, and keep on being Anna's friend. Someday, God willing, she'd show she really did like him.

And someday, she might trust him enough that he could tell her the truth and know she'd *still* like him.

Anna came downstairs from working in her studio and stopped half-way when voices carried up to her. Luke, speaking Spanish to Josh.

Her breath caught at the sound of his deep mellow voice as the words rolled easily from his tongue. Two matching dark heads leaned together at the dining table over Josh's school work.

He'd wanted to be with Luke every day since going back to school after Spring break. Luke took over driving him to school in Orchard Bridge and picking him up, fitting his building work around that. He helped Josh with homework. They walked Pattie Pork Pie together. She hadn't needed to ask Luke to clean Pattie's quarters again, he'd done it anyway.

Inevitably, Josh begged permission for Luke to stay to dinner then get him ready for bed. She'd started cooking for three. Luke left as soon as Josh was in bed. No time alone together, apart from showing him out the door.

Thankfully, Dan made sure to tell Tabby that Luke was back with him in the church house by nine every night, killing any gossip. No one could claim he lived with them. The worst that could be said was that Luke was making up for lost time with his son.

They knew they weren't doing anything wrong.

God knew they weren't doing anything wrong.

But in a town like Sweetapple Falls, they had to be seen not doing anything wrong.

She should feel happy Luke spent so much time with Josh. The boy almost glowed with happiness. Having him around helped her, too.

The house and the van were the best she'd ever seen them. Her chronic backache from hauling the ramps in and out of the van for the school run had vanished. Josh preferred homework to computer games, now Luke did it with him.

She'd even been able to get more paintings done, a huge help for their finances. In tourist season, they sold faster than she could paint, and she needed a stockpile in case Josh won through to the next round of Talent Trek and they had to go on tour.

But having Luke around was hard, too. Every time Josh called Luke Dad, regret for the lost years hit her. Worse, the more time she spent around Luke, the harder it got to stay cool and distant, the way she wanted to.

They both looked up as she came into the room. Josh burst into eager talk about what they'd been doing, but it was Luke her eyes clung to, no matter how she tried to force her gaze away.

His slow easy smile made her tummy turn over.

She could do it. Concentrate. Keep things matter of fact. Stop her voice trembling like a schoolgirl around him.

"Almost time for dinner, guys. Would you clear the table for me?"

"I think we're done, aren't we, cowboy?" Luke's smile and tone held obvious affection.

Please God, don't let him leave and break Josh's heart. She quickly suppressed the added, *Or mine.*

Her heart was fine. Just fine.

CHAPTER TWELVE

ANNA TOLD HERSELF SHE needed to stay stronger, that was all. Escaping into the kitchen to check the casserole she'd put in the oven earlier gave the perfect excuse to get away.

The savory aroma as she lifted the lid should make her feel hungry, but elephants rather than butterflies rampaged in her stomach when Luke was around. Elephants who didn't do much for her appetite.

"Smells good," he said behind her.

She dropped the spoon she had ready to stir the stew and pressed a hand to her thumping chest. "Don't sneak up on me like that!" At least she could pretend surprise made her heart race, and not his nearness.

He picked the spoon up, put it in the sink, and handed her a new one. He already knew his way around her kitchen, opening the right drawer. While she put the rolls in the oven to heat through, he collected what they'd need to set the table.

It all seemed so domesticated, so ordinary.

So like the life she'd hoped they'd have together.

Pointless if-onlys racked her. They couldn't redo the past, and they'd be crazy to try.

During the meal, her glance kept straying his direction. She forced herself to look away and concentrate on Josh's chatter. She'd only been half listening, distracted by Luke.

"Can Luke come too, Mom? Pur-leez?" Josh asked.

Last time she'd been paying attention, he'd been talking about

Power Soccer and the upcoming games. If Luke wanted to take that over, dropping being a soccer mom now and then was fine with her. "Sure, honey," she said.

Josh lifted his clenched fists in a victory salute and beamed. "We'll get their wheelchair accessible family suite. It's just like an apartment. If we room together, Dad, you can help me so Mom doesn't have to." He grinned up at her, clearly proud of himself. "That way it can be a holiday for you, Mom."

Startled, she looked from one to the other. What had she just agreed to? She didn't want to admit she'd been so busy trying not to go too moony over Luke that she hadn't tuned in to what Josh actually asked.

"I never thought you'd say yes," Josh piped, with a huge smile. "You're the best, Mom! It'll be even more fun skiing with Luke there."

Anna's tummy clenched. She raised her hands to her face and rubbed her eyes. She'd just agreed to spend an entire weekend away with Luke. How could she get through it?

But how could she not get through it? The joy on Josh's face told her there was no way she could back out now. And the flutter of her heart at the hope on Luke's made her wonder if she truly wanted to.

"I'm happy to help you, Josh," he said. "But I'll get a separate room. Your mom and I shouldn't stay in the same suite. Not when we're not married."

Josh started up in his chair, a wide I-have-an-idea grin spreading on his face.

Luke forestalled what she feared Josh planned to say, holding up a hand. "And no, we can't get married before the trip, just so we can share a suite."

Josh subsided into his chair. "Awww. You could if you both wanted to. How long does it take to get married in Oregon? I can look it up for you?"

"Forget it, Josh." Her determined tone should tell him she meant it.

"I haven't forgotten your promise. That you'd marry the man I wanted for my dad." His lip jutted mulishly. Then he lifted his thin shoulders in a shrug, and smiled. "Luke told me that would take time. At least he's coming with us. That's enough for now."

Luke's glance at her, holding a mix of apology and laughter, suggested he was as surprised as she was by Josh's question and her response.

Thankfully, he recognized they needed to do all they could avoid any more gossip.

And avoid temptation.

She could safely ignore that inner whisper. No danger of being tempted into anything she shouldn't do. After being burned once, she'd make sure to keep her distance, all weekend.

Something hopeful lifted in Luke's chest when Anna agreed to the ski trip. He'd been so sure she'd say no. Then shock had widened her eyes and she'd stiffened, covering her face. When she'd lowered her hands, the smile firmly pinned in place wasn't quite convincing.

She'd said yes without knowing what she'd agreed to.

He loosed a long slow breath. Foolish to hope. Clearly, the last thing she wanted was him on the trip, but she wouldn't disappoint Josh by saying so.

He couldn't disappoint Josh either.

"Thank you for letting me join in the trip. I haven't skied since I was younger than Josh, but I loved it then." He smiled, as if she'd intended to invite him along. It seemed the best way to manage things.

She nodded, her hint of an eye roll and a rueful twist of the lips making it clear she knew that he knew she hadn't meant to agree.

He couldn't figure her out. Sometimes she couldn't get away from him fast enough. Other times, he caught her watching him with a sweet surprising glow in her eyes. All he could do was pray, not rush her, and trust in God's will.

After dinner, Josh wheeled full-speed to the computer. "It's only ten days away. We have to book straight away so we don't miss out."

Luke met Anna's eyes over Josh's head. Staying available for Josh stopped her having a regular job. That didn't make for a reliable cash flow. "I'd like to pay for the trip."

She raised her chin, in that stubborn, determined way she'd developed in the last twelve years. "No. You already paid, by fixing the roof for us."

No point arguing with her. She'd only get even more resistant. Let her pay for herself and Josh. She couldn't stop him paying for his own room, and he'd make sure to pick up the bill for gas, meals, and any other extras.

Once he had Josh exercised and tucked in for the night, Luke returned to the kitchen. Anna waited at the back door, hand on the lock, ready to open it for him.

So obviously eager to see him gone.

Luke reached to stop her, touching her arm, and she stilled. Something unspoken passed between them as their gazes met. His chest tightened. The warmth and depth in Anna's eyes told him the truth, beyond any doubt.

Despite her avoidance tactics, she felt the same for him as he did for her. Could it be fear of being hurt again that made her fight it, resist being around him?

He'd felt she rejected him by deciding to let Josh be adopted, so he'd run. But she saw that as him abandoning her. Then both her parents died, leaving her alone with Josh. It made a kind of crazy sense that she'd want to stay independent and not let anyone help her.

If he could be patient, give her time to believe he'd stay this time, eventually they'd get to a place where she trusted him. Where he could open up about the past.

And maybe she'd understand, forgive him, give him the second chance with her he longed for. The chance to regain the trust and affection of the one woman he'd ever loved.

The possibility flooded his heart with wild joy, like a gift of grace, a promise from God.

Somehow, he dragged air into his lungs and managed to speak as if nothing had happened, and that single touch and glance hadn't been an epiphany. "I'm sorry you're stuck with me on the trip. I know you'd rather I didn't come. But we have to follow through, for Josh."

Her polite smile bent at the edges, and she pulled her arm away from his hand. "That will teach me to pay more attention to Josh's chatter, won't it?" She shrugged. "We'll manage. It's important he gets to do the things he wants to, while he's well enough."

Her voice broke, but not before he heard the desolation lurking behind her brave words.

Something in Luke broke too. Anna had explained enough of

Josh's condition and he'd read enough on the Internet to know things could only get worse. One day, Anna would need to grieve another huge loss.

When she did, he wanted to be there for her.

She held the door open. "Just go now. We'll get through it, for Josh's sake. He's all that matters."

Luke held back the words he longed to tell her.

Josh matters, yes. I'm glad to be his father. But God brought me here for more than that. And you're more than his mother. You matter too. Rebuilding our love matters.

But he said nothing, and walked out the open door.

She wasn't ready to hear that yet. Maybe, she'd never be.

Ten days later, Luke parked the van outside the rustic timber ski lodge, hauled Josh's ramps into place, and waited for him to steer his way out of the van.

Anna surprised him by dropping her usual I-can-do-it attitude. She let him drive the four hours to Mount Eastwood. Despite a strong sense of gritted teeth, she seemed determined to be cheerful.

Since agreeing to the trip, they'd inevitably been together, doing things with Josh. He'd caught her watching him more than once, but she'd made sure they were never alone for more than a few seconds when she shooed him out the door after Josh's bedtime or when he dropped the van off after taking Josh to school.

That was okay.

God gave him the gift of that moment in the kitchen to remind him to be patient. He prayed that time would show her it was safe to trust him again.

He'd kept busy, done all he could to help with Josh, and tried not to mind the way she so obviously sidestepped him every time he came near.

Josh jiggled in his chair, bursting with anticipation. "It's amazing. Even better than I expected."

It was. The boughs of the nearby pines sparkled with ice crystals. The snow covered mountains gleaming in the hazy sunlight took Luke's breath away just as much as the cold crisp air tickling his nose. But sadness tinged his awe at God's creation.

Being here reminded him painfully of his mom. Of how his childhood could have been, if it wasn't for the drugs she'd valued more than him.

He pushed those thoughts away. Josh and Anna were his focus now.

Wide eyed, Josh pointed to the huge cable car ski lift, less than a hundred yards from them. "That must be how they get my chair up the mountain. When can we go? Straight away?"

Luke understood Josh's excitement. He wanted to get out on the snow again himself.

Even more, he wanted to see Josh fulfill a dream.

"Slow down, cowboy. No eat, no ski. That's the rule. We'll check into our rooms, have lunch, *then* ride up. Your lesson isn't until one thirty."

Josh pretended to pout. "You old folk need to rest, I guess."

Anna waved a hand in a fake slap. "Enough of that old folk talk. I'm still thirty for a few more months."

"And Dad's thirty-one already. That's what I mean, old." Josh grinned. "But lunch sounds good. I can meet up with the guys. Adam's already here. That's their car, over there." He waved, then powered away from them, up the wheelchair-friendly entrance ramp to the lodge.

Anna grinned and rolled her eyes a little as he zoomed off. "At least one of us will have a good weekend." She turned to the van, grabbing the handle of a suitcase.

Luke reached out to stop her. He should do the grunt work, not Anna. The sleeve of her blue fluffy sweater yielded softly beneath his hand. The sunlight touched her glowing face as she turned to him, a question in her eyes, lips parted a little. He longed to kiss her, so much. It would be easy to lean closer...

But kissing her again would be a bad idea.

Patience. Wait, and trust in God's perfect timing.

Lifting his hand from her arm, he stepped back. "Let me do this. You go with Josh. We want this weekend to be a holiday for you."

For a moment, she looked set to challenge him. Then she shrugged and smiled, a sweet smile that warmed him despite the icy air. "Okay. Just this once, you win."

As she followed Josh into the lodge, something in the jaunty way she walked suggested she knew he watched her go.

He smiled as he unloaded their cases.

A man came out with a baggage cart, his smile brightening eyes half-hidden beneath a thatch of graying hair. "Welcome to Mount Eastwood. I'm Bill Bates, the manager. Let me help you with those."

They shifted the luggage, and joined Anna and Josh inside the bright, welcoming lodge, all natural wood and big windows. The friendly manager checked them in then showed them to their rooms. With two bedrooms and a huge accessible bathroom, the family apartment looked perfect for Anna and Josh. A fireplace loaded with logs ready to be lit waited in the living room. Luke's smaller room was down the hall.

Josh's glance around the suite took all of a nano-second. "This is great." His hand shifted on his chair control, moving him to the open door. "So can we have lunch now?"

Anna and Luke's eyes met, laughing at his eagerness. As they did, something inside Luke shifted. They felt like a family.

Josh rushed them through lunch and straight to choosing ski clothes, more interested in getting on the slopes than being with his friends. If his lessons today went well, he and his instructor would ski alongside his able-bodied buddies tomorrow. Impatience bounced him in his chair as Luke and Anna tried their ski legs on the gentle slope next to the lodge.

To his surprise, Luke's body remembered how. It only took a few passes for him to be skiing like he hadn't been away from the slopes. Gliding over the snow again brought something deeply buried in him alive.

His lost childhood? He breathed thanks to God for this one sweet loving memory of his mom.

Anna seemed far less comfortable. Shaking her head, she sat down on the low log fence at the edge of the car park, where Josh waited.

Luke skied over to her. "What's wrong?"

She gazed up at him, her cheeks pale. "Dad always told me I never could ski, and he was right. I hate feeling out of control." Her hands lowered to unclip her skis. "I should stay off the snow and just watch you guys. If I go with you, I'll slow you down. I'm too afraid of falling."

His lips tightened. Anna's father had a lot to answer for. The Deputy brought her up to play it safe, never take a risk. The only risk she'd taken in her life was falling for him.

Though look how that worked out. Could it be, her dad was right?

Then he glanced at Josh, and couldn't regret their past. He needed to trust God brought them together for a reason. Then, and now.

"I doubt his instructor will take Josh off the easy green-grade slopes today. Would you try? If you give it a go then feel you can't, I'll ski you back to the cafe at the top of the lift." He prayed as he spoke, hoping he wasn't pressuring her.

Sudden insight told him Anna trusted herself as little as she did him. Her determination to stay in control covered fear, as surely as the snow blanketed the ground around them.

"Come on, Mom!" Josh jiggled his chair controls.

Anna stood, pasting on a strained smile. "I'll do my best. If I can't ski with you, I'll cheer from the sidelines."

Josh rushed them onto the gondola, swinging them above the snow as it carried them part-way up the mountain. With barely a glance at the spectacular view from the station, he powered straight to the Adaptive Center.

By the time Luke collected his and Anna's skis from the gondola's rack, Josh had already found his instructor. He waved his arms as he talked enthusiastically to a tall, sandy-haired man.

Luke and Anna hurried over.

"This is Dane, my instructor. He's going to figure out what sort of ski chair I need. It's so awesome." Excitement lit Josh's thin face.

Luke ran a measuring eye over the instructor's unruly hair and baggy clothing. He didn't look far into his twenties. Out on the slopes, they'd hand responsibility for their son to this man, so he'd better be trustworthy. If Josh was injured on this trip, he'd never forgive himself.

And Anna would never forgive him, either.

.

CHAPTER THIRTEEN

DESPITE HIS CONCERN FOR JOSH, Luke had to chuckle.

Dane's reassuring smile and firm handshake suggested he knew exactly what Luke was thinking. "I'm a trained adaptive ski instructor. I've done this for the last five years. My sister is in a wheelchair, and Dad trusts me to take her out. I'll take good care of Josh, exactly the same as I would for her. Ready to go?"

Josh's beaming grin left no one in any doubt how eager he was. Luke nodded. His gut instinct told him to trust Dane. Anna's smaller nod held more reluctance.

Luke wanted to reach out, hold her hand to encourage her. But chances were, that would make things worse.

Dane led them to a hut filled with equipment, where he assessed Josh then strapped him into what he called a sit ski. The bucket-shaped seat and tubular metal frame resting on two skis, with a handlebar and reins attached to the back, looked way too flimsy. Luke prayed it was safe.

"I'll give you outriggers, special ski poles so you can help steer." Dane held up a helmet. "You must wear this. That's compulsory, okay?"

Josh stopped his excited rocking long enough for Dane to fit the helmet, along with goggles to cover his glasses. He waved the short poles Dane handed him, with miniature skis on the ends. "When do I get to ski."

Dane laughed. "Right now." He attached the chair's reins to a harness he wore, and pushed Josh in the sit ski through the back door of the hut.

Luke watched closely as the instructor taught Josh simple balance exercises and how to use the outriggers on flat snow without moving. His tension released as he saw Dane wasn't going to let Josh's enthusiasm and impatience overrule safety.

When Dane announced Josh was ready to move to a slope, seeing the kid's jubilant grin felt like being handed a million dollars. Luke turned to Anna beside him and saw his joy reflected on her face.

He held back his strong urge to hug her. Sharing this moment of joy had to be enough.

"Okay if we come with you?" His question was for Josh, as much as Dane. At Josh's age, maybe he didn't want Mom and Dad always hanging around.

Josh's wide smile rewarded him. "Sure it's okay! I want you both there with me."

Luke knelt to help Anna with her skis, fastened his own, then followed as Dane pushed Josh to the top of a slight slope. Remembering when he'd learned to ski, how scary his legs sliding away from him felt, he kept as close a watch on Anna as he did on Josh.

That sensation could be terrifying, especially for someone like her, who put so much importance on staying in control.

Dane threw Anna an assessing glance. "Mom, Dad, I don't know how much you've skied before. One bit of advice. If you feel like you're losing balance, try to keep your arms in front of you, and where you can see them. And hold in your stomach muscles. That'll help you regain balance."

Luke smiled and nodded, feeling better about all this. If the instructor saw Anna's nervousness and took time to reassure her, he'd be fine with Josh.

"Here we go, Josh, your first run." Dane grinned at the excited boy. "Don't try to steer yet, just rest the outriggers on the snow and get your balance." He let the sit ski move forward, keeping his grip on the handles. It glided down the slope, then stopped by itself at the bottom, where the ground leveled.

"I did it!" Josh shouted. "I skied!"

"You sure did, cowboy!" Elation warmed Luke's chest. Anna's glowing face showed she felt it, too.

A few more runs, some practice steering, and Dane announced

Josh was ready for a longer slope. Fear for Josh tremored through Luke, but he couldn't argue in the face of Dane's quiet confidence and Josh's delight. He looked to Anna, asking with his eyes if she felt up to more.

She nodded decisively. "I've got to be there to watch Josh conquer the mountain. Wouldn't miss it for anything." Her smile wobbled a little at the edges.

Pride in her swelled Luke's heart, seeing her love for their son defeat her fear.

Love could always defeat fear, if we chose to let it.

Dane maneuvered Josh in his sit ski to the magic carpet ground-level lift, taking them higher up the slope. Luke and Anna followed, skiing alongside Dane and Josh for run after run.

Josh's glee and fearless insistence they go higher and faster thrilled him as much as the rush of wind and snow. Despite the skill and strength it must take to manage the sit ski when Josh could do little to control it, Dane seemed equally tireless. Luke's muscles protested against the unaccustomed movement, and all he did was ski.

Anna's set expression suggested she enjoyed it far less than he and Josh did, but every time he asked if she wanted to stop, she refused.

"Last run," Dane warned Josh as they came to a halt at the bottom.

Josh grimaced, but nodded his head. "I guess so. We've done a lot." He grinned. "Going fast feels good as I hoped. My wheelchair is so slow."

Luke's heart twisted for Josh. While his friends whizzed around him on bicycles and skateboards, his chair's top speed was four miles an hour. Tomorrow, Josh could ski with his buddies, and for once come near keeping up.

"We'll make this last run a good one," Dane said. They rode the magic carpet as far as it went, then he pushed Josh to the top of the steepest slope yet. "See your friends, over there? Let's beat them down the mountain."

Luke looked down. This run was higher and longer than any they'd done before. He threw Dane a worried glance, not wanting to ask out loud if he was sure it was safe for Josh. The smile and nod he got in return reassured him.

What about Anna? Her tense lips, pale face, and white-knuckled grip on her ski poles held far less confidence, yet she seemed determined. "I can do it."

"You two ski behind us, so you have more room to move." Dane said. "Don't feel you need to keep up. Ski in long curves rather than a straight line. You're more in control that way."

Luke trusted Dane knew what he was doing. Whispering a prayer for all their safety, he hoped Anna would manage. A reassuring smile for her, a quick touch of her hand through gloves, and she gave a decisive nod. They pushed off, and flew down the mountain behind Josh and Dane, in a heart-pounding adrenaline rush.

As they slowed to a halt, Josh was almost incoherent with glee. "Did you see? We overtook the guys! I went faster than them!"

Being part of Josh's triumph flooded Luke with jubilation. Ready to explode like Fourth of July fireworks with love and pride, he hugged Josh, at the same moment Anna did. Arms entangled, they hugged their son together, sharing his joy.

He'd never felt more love for her. This was how it should be, how he'd wanted it all along. He and Anna and Josh, together. In this moment, they were a family.

Josh's friends caught up and crowded around, and they let him go.

Luke's eyes met Anna's and held, in an intense gaze shimmering with awareness. The amazing woman she'd grown into snatched his breath away just as strongly as the ski run had. But with all that lay between them, they had to climb a mountain far steeper than the one they'd just skied down before she'd open her heart to him again.

Anna struggled to make small talk with the other parents during the restaurant dinner Luke insisted on paying for that evening. Everyone laughed and moaned about unaccustomed aches and pains. She tried to join in, despite the tension stretching her tight.

Concern for Josh wasn't the problem. On the kids' table, he chattered away to his friends, still buzzing with excitement. His usual bubbliness paled in comparison to today's mood. She'd rarely seen him quite so happy and animated.

And she knew why. It was more than just the skiing.

Luke.

Having his father there made all the difference for Josh. And for her. Luke's presence brought joy to their son, but stole her appetite and tightened her tummy.

His gentle attentiveness unraveled her resolve to keep him at arm's length. Too many times, they'd exchanged looks or touches, declaring louder than words ever could that they'd become closer than she'd intended.

Tonight, he pulled out her chair for her, passed things before she asked, made her feel thoroughly taken care of. They probably looked every inch as much a married couple as anyone else at the parents' table.

Perhaps more so, judging by slightly envious glances from some of the wives.

Conflicting emotions rocked her. They weren't a couple, though she got the feeling Luke wanted them to be. She'd thought she knew what she wanted. A quiet, peaceful life, giving Josh the best she could, without getting involved with Luke.

But today, she couldn't be so sure.

The warm intensity in his blue gaze roused memories of him promising to love her forever. If he'd really only left her after Josh was born because he felt rejected and believed she didn't want him, rather than because he didn't want her, it made a difference. A big difference.

Her safe, secure, almost-under-control life as a single mom seemed years in the past, not just weeks.

She'd kept her balance on the ski slopes today, overcome her fear of falling. But Luke could knock her off balance, in a fall far worse than any skiing fall. What if she overcome her fear of falling for Luke, letting herself depend on him, only to be left alone again?

Keeping her heart closed to him was the only safe choice.

Anything else held danger. Yet as their fingers accidentally brushed and awareness of him shook her, safety didn't look nearly so appealing.

After dinner, Josh's adrenaline rush wore off, and he slumped. Luke insisted he go to bed early, ready for another day's skiing tomorrow. He also insisted she relax, while he did Josh's bedtime care.

A shower unknotted her muscles a little. But when she walked into the apartment's living room, her tension returned in an instant. The fire crackled in the rough-hewn stone fireplace, and Luke stood at the kitchenette with his back to her.

He turned with a smile that sent her senses into overdrive. She sank into the sofa and watched the flames dance, trying to still her dancing pulses and keep her eyes off Luke.

"Bill came in to start the fire while you were in the bathroom. I made you tea." He placed a steaming mug on the low table in front of her. "I'll finish up with Josh now."

She risked looking up at him. "Thank you. I could get used to being pampered like this."

"You deserve it. Josh and I wanted you to get a chance to relax this weekend." She'd tried to joke, but his reply sounded sincere.

He smiled that nerve-jangling smile again as he went into Josh's room. Her heart jumped. How could she relax, when Luke's nearness put her every sense on high alert?

She lifted the mug, and a spiced vanilla aroma drifted to her. Her favorite chai. He must have brought the tea bags with him. Sipping the milky sweetness, she couldn't deny she enjoyed the way Luke made her feel so cherished.

A noise from Josh's room pulled her to the edge of the chair. A groan, followed by laughter. His stretches. She tried to sink back into the sofa, but her muscles refused to obey.

Letting someone else take over Josh's care still didn't come easy.

Especially Luke. Josh's father should be the natural one to help him. But she couldn't believe it would last, even as her heart told her again and again she should give Luke a chance.

Confusion drove her to pray.

Lord, show me what I'm supposed to do about Luke. I don't know how safe it is to let myself believe in this.

The door opened and Luke came out. "Ready to say goodnight?"

If only she could stop that fizzing rush at the sight of him and the sound of his voice.

In Josh's room, she checked Luke had done everything right. He had, with the same care and attention he gave to everything else, from working on the van to the church building work to remembering to grab her tea bags from the kitchen.

Josh grinned up at her sleepily.

"Goodnight, Mister. It's been a big day for you," she said, resting a hand on his thin shoulder, then kissing her other hand and patting it quickly on his forehead.

What she really wanted to do was give him a big hug and never let him go. Honesty forced her to admit it would be more to comfort herself than him. Chances were, if she tried, he'd squirm away with an embarrassed, "Aw, Mom."

Letting him grow apart from her and turn to his father instead was hard. But for his sake, she had to let him go. And she had to accept Luke was part of their lives.

"It's been the awesomest day ever," Josh murmured. "Mom, Dad, thanks so much." His voice trailed off and his eyelids lowered.

She stood next to his bed beside Luke, watching their son together, as Josh drifted into sleep. The intimacy of the simple act jolted her. How many nights had she longed for Luke to be there with them, helping her with Josh?

And now he was.

Her attention shifted from Josh to the man standing so close to her. Luke's slow steady breathing filled her ears, over-riding Josh's quiet sighing breaths. Instead of Josh's freshly showered baby powder scent, the tang of Luke's soap and sunscreen filled her nostrils.

Her skin tingled as if even her tiniest hairs were drawn towards him.

Despite all the years that had passed, she hadn't let another man close since Luke. She hadn't wanted to. No one stirred the feelings in her Luke did.

His nearness became something she couldn't pretend to ignore. She stepped away from him, into the lounge where she could put more space between them.

Sitting on the sofa, she could kid herself that the fire's glow heated her cheeks, not her awareness of him.

He followed, leaving Josh's bedroom door half open, and moved to the mantelpiece to stare into the flames. The flickering light danced on his hair, bringing out the auburn in its rich brown. As he leaned forward to put another log on the fire, a heavy lock flopped forward over his face.

Longing rose in her to touch his hair, to bury her fingers in it and draw him closer.

Luke looked up from the fire. Something in the way his eyes reflected the glimmering intensity of the flames made her stomach clench and her heart jump in her chest. Hesitant, as if giving her time to refuse, he sat next to her on the sofa.

She should ask him to move away, should get up herself, anything to put more distance between them.

But she didn't.

Warmth, understanding, and that indefinable something more she wasn't sure she wanted to see gleamed in his gaze. She looked away, but he lifted one hand and gently turned her face toward him. Her skin tingled beneath his callused fingertips as his hand cupped her cheek and jawline.

All his movements were slow and tentative, letting her know she could stop him, any time she chose.

"Anna," he said, his low soft voice as much a caress as his touch.

She closed her eyes and bit her lower lip to stop it trembling.

Logic and everything her father taught her screamed she should pull away. But something kept her rooted in place, leaning into his hand, letting the warmth of his touch seep into her.

CHAPTER FOURTEEN

ANNA SAT STILL, her breath caught in her throat as Luke's hand cradled her face.

"Being with Josh today meant more than I can say," he murmured. "Thank you for letting me be part of it."

She couldn't move, couldn't speak, could barely breathe. Her nod was the slightest movement of her head against his hand.

The draw she felt towards Luke was far from just physical. She wanted to believe in him, believe that he'd proved himself. The way he was with Josh. His work at the church. The way everyone in town respected him. He'd become a man any boy could be proud to call his father.

And a man any woman would be proud to call her husband.

She should move away, but all her awareness centered in that place where his fingers and palm rested rough-skinned yet gentle against her cheek. Every atom of her, body, heart, mind, and soul, vibrated with the nearness of him, like a magnet drawing iron filings.

"Anna." Slowly, so slowly, he lowered his head and touched his lips to hers in a soft, undemanding kiss.

She yearned towards him, leaned into his kiss, heart flaming brightly as the fire.

Then common sense rushed in. She raised her hands to his hard chest and pushed against him, pushing herself away from the tender hands holding her face. He let her go.

It was too much. All of it.

His intensity, his sincerity, his warmth. It terrified her. She couldn't allow herself to want him the way she did. Her feelings for Luke made her weak, when for the past twelve years she'd focused on staying strong for Josh.

"No. Please. I can't, Luke. We're Josh's parents, no more. We can't be more." The whisper barely squeezed through her dry throat.

She closed her eyes. He mustn't see the emotion they'd betray. If she surrendered to his kiss and the emotions rioting in her, she'd be lost.

Not physically, they both knew where to draw the line now. But they'd go too far emotionally. She'd lose control of her feelings. She'd lose her heart to him.

If she hadn't already.

The sofa cushions shifted as he stood, and muffled footsteps thudded on the deep carpet as he walked away. The door to the hallway opened with a click. Somehow, even with tightly shut eyes, she knew he stood there in the open doorway, looking back at her.

"I'm sorry. I shouldn't have done that. This wasn't the time or the place." Regret tinged his softly spoken words. "Goodnight, Anna."

She nodded, but fear stopped her looking up at him. Too afraid of what she might glimpse in his expression. Only when she heard the door quietly close and Luke exchange greetings with another parent in the hall did she open her eyes.

Clamping down hard on the love she didn't want to admit to, she sat staring into the fire until the glowing flames subsided to embers.

Luke picked up the piece of finish timber, nailed it into place, then stood back, surveying what he and the volunteer team had achieved. Ahead of schedule, they had the church project near to completion. Soon, he'd have to make a decision about other work.

One thing he knew for sure. What he'd built with Josh and Anna was way too precious to leave.

When he'd emailed his boss Larry to quit his old job, Larry hinted there might be a new position available. Managing a long-term U.S. based project, retraining ex-prisoners in building skills while repairing the homes of those in need. If it was based within commuting distance of Sweetapple Falls, he'd grab the job with both hands.

House the World gave him so much, he wouldn't miss another opportunity to give back.

In the meantime, he'd have no trouble finding temporary work with a contracting crew. Anything that didn't take him away from Josh and Anna.

Finally, she seemed to be developing some trust in him, but he'd need to step carefully. Kissing her on Saturday night in the ski lodge was a mistake. Once again, he'd let emotion overrule sense. Her trust was too fragile, delicate as an eggshell.

He had to be patient, give her time.

And he'd gone and rushed things. Again.

In the days since, he'd made sure not to put a foot out of line. No touching. No meeting her eyes, hoping to see warmth mirrored there. No time alone together.

If Josh wasn't there, neither was he. It was the only way to play things.

So why did he want so much to reach out a hand to her and touch her shoulder or cheek as she hummed while she cooked for them in the kitchen? Why when he walked past her as she sat quietly reading in the lounge did he want to drop a kiss on top of her head? Why was his mind on her, when he should be concentrating on getting these last few boards nailed into place?

Because in every way but one, they were a real family.

He got Josh up in the morning. He took him to school. He worked all day, then picked Josh up from school. He helped with his homework. He cared for Josh's pet. They ate dinner together. After dinner, they read, watched TV, or he worked with Josh on a project while Anna baked or painted or crafted. He put Josh to bed, like any other parent would.

Then he got in the old blue pick-up he'd bought to cart building supplies, and left the two people he loved most behind, while he went back to Dan's spare room in the church house.

For all he told himself he should be thankful for what he had, he couldn't help wanting more.

Nearly time to quit here, go to Anna's to get her van, then pick Josh up from school. His cellphone beeped, and he pulled it out of his pocket to check the caller ID.

Anna's number.

Pulse accelerating, muttering a prayer for her and Josh, he

fumbled to bring up the text message. Anna had told him Josh could go from well-for-him to seriously ill in a few hours.

He read the brief message and the adrenaline drained away, leaving him wrung out.

Josh was fine.

The kid had buried himself deep in Luke's heart. He'd be shot to pieces if anything happened to his son. Thankfully, the message was just Anna asking if she could come too when he collected Josh, and if they could stop by the big supermarket in Orchard Bridge.

There went his resolution to avoid being alone with her.

He hammered home the last nail, packed away his tools and tidied the site, and headed to Anna's house to switch vehicles and collect her. They both sat silent as he drove. Saying she was overdue on a blog post about the ski trip, she typed on her phone for the entire journey.

Convenient for them both — no need to talk.

But resisting the temptation to glance sideways at her became a challenge. Once he looked at her, he'd never tear his gaze away. The heady effect of the sweet floral scent of her shampoo in the confines of the van came close to making him a road safety hazard already.

They pulled up outside Josh's school five minutes early. The schoolyard and sidewalks that would soon be teeming with kids held only a few waiting parents. Could be, them being alone together was a good thing. He had a question to ask her and he'd rather Josh didn't hear it. Here was his chance.

As soon as he parked the van, he spoke.

So did she.

"Do you mind..."

"Would you..."

After twenty minutes of near silence, they'd both spoken at once.

Although they didn't allow their eyes to connect, shared laughter broke the tension stiffening the air between them since Saturday.

"You go first," he said.

Anna sucked in an audible breath. "Josh has the semi-final for Talent Trek in Portland in two weeks and I know he wants you there so would you come with us please?" She rushed the words out in one breath, without looking at him. He almost heard her unsaid "Phew" at the end.

Clearly, it had been hard for her to ask. But she had. A good sign.

He wanted to cheer and victory punch the air. Though she looked like a startled deer, ready to bolt if he made a sudden move.

He smiled. "I was about to ask if you'd let me drive you there. I don't like the thought of you and Josh driving all that way alone. I'm guessing flying would be difficult?"

Rolling her gorgeous eyes, she held up both hands. "Don't put the idea in his head. Flying's something else on his bucket list. We might have to, if he wins this round and needs to go further. But for now, given the choice between a five hour drive and the challenges involved in getting Josh on a flight, I'll choose the drive."

"Makes sense." He kept his voice bland, showing no sign of the jubilation he felt over her willingness to include him.

She gave a tense half-smile. "Thank you for offering to drive us." She hesitated. "Will you come along to the filming as Josh's second support person too? It's a long day, and he'll be glad to have you there." Her shoulders lifted in a little shrug and her lips twisted. "We're his parents. I'm okay with you coming along, for his sake."

For Josh's sake, not hers. He needed to be satisfied that that she allowed him time with Josh. That had to be enough, for now.

Some time, he'd have to tell her about his past. Though she'd judge him. Find it hard to accept. Might not see beyond his old mistakes to see the man he was now, how God had changed him. He needed to wait until she trusted him enough to hear the truth, if that moment ever came.

The sun came out from behind a cloud, lighting her hair like a golden halo. She looked beautiful and way beyond his reach, the way she had the night they met.

That hadn't changed.

She was still beautiful, and until she knew and accepted the truth about his past, still way beyond his reach.

Anna never imagined that little more than a month after Luke turned up unwelcome and unannounced on her doorstep, they'd be in the supermarket together.

But here they were.

To anyone who saw them, her choosing groceries from the shelves, Luke pushing the shopping cart, and Josh trundling alongside offering advice on what to buy, they'd look every inch a real family. And now Luke had agreed to come to Portland with them, they'd look even more like one, and on national television, too.

At least asking him to join the trip for Talent Trek seemed to have melted some of the ice between them since the ski weekend. She knew he regretted kissing her. He'd kept everything focused on Josh since then.

She was Josh's Mom, he was Josh's Dad. Nothing more.

Exactly what she'd told him she wanted.

Except now, she wasn't so sure. Her mind was only half on her shopping list. The other half was on Luke. Constantly aware of his presence, the height of him, the breadth of him, the faint odor of sweat from a day's honest building work.

Her pulse pounded so hard the whole way to Orchard Bridge, every word she wrote for the blog post was probably gibberish.

But despite the workout her heart got around him, she could get used to this.

They circulated the aisles, filling the trolley high. Luke pretended to strain to push it. "I want to pay for this. You wouldn't be buying half this much if I wasn't eating with you and Josh most evenings."

Anna tensed. Yes, the food he ate cost money, but accepting help from others stuck in her craw. Even help from Luke.

It felt too much like being dependent on him.

Pushing the cart for them was one thing, paying for their groceries was something else. She'd already let him do so much.

She risked getting used to being looked after, thinking of him as permanent. He'd been great so far, but the building work at the church was nearly done. He hadn't said a word about what he'd do once that was done.

"No." She shook her head to emphasize the point. "You've done so much for us, fixing up the house and van. I'm not accepting money from you."

Luke shook his head right back at her. "I eat food, I pay for food. It's as simple as that. And Josh's expenses are as much my responsibility as yours." He grinned. "Anyway, I have control of the shopping cart. Race you to the checkout." He pushed against the cart like a sprinter under starter's orders, looking back at her with a spark in his eyes.

She didn't argue. The glow warming Luke's gaze warmed her, too.

She liked feeling his approval. And it was easier not to fight. Her hands went up in surrender. "You win. This time."

He punched the air, grinning.

"Next time, of course, I'll simply do my marketing by myself." She smiled her triumph.

Josh's head turned from one to the other like a spectator at a tennis game as they sparred, eyes wide behind his glasses.

Luke appealed to him. "So tell me, Josh. Who won?"

Her traitor son laughed. "You won this round, Dad. She'll let you pay for sure rather than make a fuss at the checkout." Then he winked at her, so cute she couldn't help laughing. "Though Mom will win next time. Mom always wins in the end."

"I think that makes it a draw," Luke said. His smile made her stomach flip. "Is this all the shopping?"

They made their way to the front of the store, and Luke paid for the groceries. Josh's gaze fixed on a boy about his age, further down the store. The tense way his hands clasped the arms of his chair told her he was worried.

"What's wrong?" she asked.

"It's someone from my class, I think he stole something," he whispered.

"We need to tell the manager and get them to call the police."

"No, Mom," Josh protested. "I don't want to get him in trouble." He looked up at Luke. "Dad, please go talk to him. That kid in the red shirt. His name is Richard. I saw him put a magazine in his bag."

Luke stilled, and his face paled beneath his tan. He sucked in a loud breath.

"I think the police should deal with this," she said. "Dad always said thieves were the lowest of the low. If he's stolen something, he should be punished. It's the only way he'll learn not to do it again."

"Until he takes it out of the store without paying, it's not theft." Luke frowned. "I'll talk to him."

He squared his shoulders and marched over to the boy. They were too far away to hear what Luke said, but the boy pulled a magazine from his school bag. His shoulders slumped and his head hung low as he handed it over.

She expected Luke to return it to the rack. Instead, unbelievably, he took the magazine to the cash register, paid for it, and gave it back to the boy. It felt so wrong.

"That's no way to teach him not to steal. You rewarded him for bad behavior." She exploded as soon as Luke was near enough to hear her angry whispered words. "What's to stop him stealing again?"

Luke closed his eyes, and his shoulders sagged just like the boy's had. When he opened his eyes, sadness and weariness dulled them.

"He's not a criminal. He's a kid who made a stupid mistake. A random act of kindness can have more effect than punishment. The knowledge that next time it might not be a classmate who sees him steal will stop him. I warned him it could be the store detective or an off-duty police officer." His smile looked more like a grimace. "Or a responsible citizen like you, who knows it's her duty to hand him over to the manager. I don't think he'll steal again."

"Thanks, Dad." Josh looked at him gratefully, like he was a hero.

She wasn't so sure. She'd been brought up to believe wrongdoing deserved punishment. Her father's punishment had been stopping loving her, when she did wrong. Like when she'd fallen for Luke and come home pregnant.

Didn't that teach her not to make the same mistake again?

Surely it did. Her head told her she wouldn't fall in love with Luke again. Trouble was, her heart told her something different.

So all that meant was she needed to be stronger, listen to her head more.

She could do it. She had to.

CHAPTER FIFTEEN

ANNA COULDN'T LET HERSELF soften toward Luke any more. She just couldn't.

And now she had a good reason not to. Luke let the boy off far too lightly. It didn't sit comfortably with her to know the thief escaped the punishment he deserved.

"Dad's approach was the right one. He wouldn't charge a kid the first time, but he made sure they understood the consequences of what they did. He'd lock them up till their parents arrived. He called it scaring them straight."

Luke looked ready to argue the point, but his cellphone rang. He glanced at the screen, and excused himself to answer it. His tight posture relaxed as he nodded and smiled through the conversation.

Clearly someone he was happier to talk to than her.

As he ended the call, he looked at Anna, then Josh. A questioning crease to his brow suggested he weighed up whether to tell them or not.

Josh, being Josh, asked straight out. "Something good?"

A wide grin spread across Luke's face. "The best. I've been on paid leave since I got here, but now the church work's done I knew I'd have to look for another job. And I have one." He put his hands together and touched them to his lips, as if giving thanks.

Anna stiffened, braced to hear the worst.

This was it then. She'd feared all along that once the church work was done, Luke would be gone, out of their lives again. She glanced at Josh. It would break his heart to lose his father now.

But surely Luke wouldn't smile like that if he was leaving them.

Luke lowered his hands. "My boss mentioned there was a chance I could work for House the World here in the U.S., for a new service they're starting."

She held her breath, waiting for the rest.

"They've offered me the job, and decided that as Orchard Bridge is on the highway and has an airport, the office for the new program can be based here. And I won't be a team member, like I expected. They want me to lead."

Luke looked like he'd been handed the world on a plate. His smile reminded her where Josh got his light-up-the-room grin from. She might have been smiling just as wide herself.

"I'll need to do some regular travel, locating managers to run local projects and doing fundraising work. But this will be my base, and I'll be here most of the time. They'll even give me leave to go on tour with Josh." Joy rang in his voice.

He'd called Sweetapple Falls home. He'd be working locally. Anna closed her eyes as joy pulsed though her.

Maybe she could believe. Maybe, she could trust he really would stay this time. The idea of trusting anyone, even Luke, still worried her sick.

But she had to try.

Anna recognized that something tight and hard in her let go once Luke told her about his new job. Everything between them felt different, though nothing had actually changed.

A week later, things really *were* different. The church build officially completed, Luke asked her to come to Orchard Bridge when he took Josh to school, and help him find an office.

Sensible move. She knew the area. They were purely doing what was best for the charity.

Even so, while Luke helped Josh with his morning routine, she took extra care getting dressed. Put on a nice impress-the-Realtor suit, hanging in her wardrobe unworn since she left her last job. Styled her hair with a few extra waves. Wore heeled pumps instead of her usual flats.

The appreciation in Luke's eyes when he looked up from Josh's computer as she came downstairs warmed her far more than it should. Telling herself she'd done it for House the World, not him, didn't help settle her jumbled emotions.

"Wow, you look the business, Mom," Josh said. "They'll want to add an extra zero to the rent."

"I hope not, House the World can't afford it." Luke flickered her a wink that made her catch her breath. He looked pretty good himself, in a borrowed suit. "Thanks for doing this, Anna. You'll be a huge help."

"Mom will find the right place for your office." Josh beamed proudly. Then he looked back to his computer, frowning. "We're looking at hotel rooms for the Talent Trek semi-final. Mom, do you mind if I room with Dad this time?"

Anna waited for the usual pang of jealousy. It didn't happen.

"Sure. I'm fine with that. Having a room of my own and the chance of some me time in Portland could be nice." She hoped her smile told Josh she still loved him, but recognized his need to grow up.

"Josh tells me they only allow for one parent to travel with underage performers. I'd like to pay half the costs, as I'm going too." Luke clearly expected her to protest.

She moved behind him to look at the computer screen, suppressing the urge to rest a hand on his shoulder. Even the discounted price at the hotel the producers asked contestants to stay at extinguished any desire to argue her independence. They'd have plenty of other expenses on the trip.

It was plain good sense to agree.

Not weakness. Not a sign she'd come to rely on Luke.

Josh chattered the whole way to his school. Just as he'd done when they'd collected him and shopped together the other day, he seemed proud to have Mom *and* Dad drop him off. He wanted them to be a family.

The other night, while Luke was out the room, Josh asked her again to marry Luke. Reminded her once more of her joking comment the night Luke came back into their lives, when she said she'd marry the man he wanted for his father.

Josh wanted Luke, and he refused to believe her promise was a joke.

She given a half-answer, and thankfully Josh dropped the topic in front of Luke. But she'd seen his gaze on them as they did things together. She knew how badly he wanted it.

That wasn't a good enough reason to get married, was it?

Not that Luke had asked her to marry him. Since that night at the ski lodge, he hadn't made any move to kiss her again. Hadn't made any attempt to get her alone.

She sensed something bothered him, but had no idea what.

"How far is the Realtor's office?" Luke asked, after they saw Josh power his chair through the school gates.

"Not far, it's down on Main Street."

He smiled. "I thought we could park the van here and walk." He glanced down at her shoes. "If that's okay?"

"Of course."

They set off toward the first Realtor she'd set up an appointment with. Only the sunny spring day and the unaccustomed heels put an extra sashay in her steps, not Luke's nearness. She didn't *really* want to reach out and take his hand and swing it like they used to when they dated.

Surely not.

When they reached the Realtor's, Anna was glad she'd dressed up. She couldn't help noticing the extra warmth in the woman's eyes when they rested on Luke, and the way she smoothed her hands down her smart red suit when she stood to shake hands. Or the way she checked them both for wedding rings.

A "He's mine" prickle of possessiveness startled Anna.

She had no right to feel that. She'd been the one who wanted to keep things strictly Mom and Dad between them. But she couldn't deny a spark of pleasure at the disappointment flickering in the Realtor's eyes when Luke placed a warm hand on her back to guide her to a seat.

The first office Sandra showed them was dingy, dark, and gloomy, over a shop on Main Street and up a narrow flight of stairs. They exchanged glances, and both shook their heads.

As they followed the Realtor down the stairs, Anna whispered to Luke. "They always show the worst one first, to make the next ones look better."

"Pray the next one is better," Luke muttered, too low for Sandra to overhear. "It couldn't be worse."

It was better.

Off Main Street in a quiet tree lined road, at the back of a huge Victorian house converted into business suites, the small ground floor office had disabled access, its own parking space, and was freshly painted a warm cream. Sunlight flooded through south-facing windows. Just being in the room lifted her spirits. Luke looked at her, and she nodded.

"What's the rental on this one?" Luke asked.

His relieved smile at the figure Sandra mentioned, though higher than the last office, suggested it was still within budget. "I don't think we need look any further. I'm ready to start the paperwork."

If Anna needed proof Luke truly intended to stay, she had it. She couldn't keep a grin off her face. But after they left Sandra's office, Luke wasn't as bouncy about securing the perfect office as she expected. Too quiet, and a troubled crease formed between his brows.

Her breathing hitched. She should have known better than to think things were going right. Whenever she thought that, things went wrong.

"What's bothering you?"

He covered his lips with a loose fist and closed his eyes for a moment before he spoke. "I want to buy that painting of yours I admired my first day in town. It would be perfect for the big bare wall in the main office. But I'm not sure it's ethical to use the charity's money for that, and I can't quite stretch to it myself."

Relief flooded her. She shook her head and laughed. "Is that all? I thought there was a problem. I can loan the painting. Or gift it to the charity and claim the tax deduction. That would cover the cost of my materials."

"Loan it."

She must have shown her surprise at the firmness of his reply.

"I want to buy that painting for myself, as soon as I can," he explained. "The new job comes with a pay rise, so I'll be able to afford it after a few months. We'll put a note on the wall telling visitors where they can see your work. And I've been thinking, you need a wider audience than you're getting in the diner. Will you let me set up a website for your art? Josh and I could do it together for his Computer Studies project."

That he'd thought of it warmed her. Told her what a secret part of her heart wanted so badly to believe was true, no matter what her head said.

Luke was staying. And he cared.

The following week, at the *Talent Trek* semi-final in Portland, Luke watched Josh carefully for signs of fatigue.

He felt limp as the lettuce in the leftover sandwiches on the catering stand. Judging by Anna's wilted posture, slumped in the hard plastic chair, she felt the same. But hyped at being close to the live filming, Josh showed no sign of flagging.

"You should have seen the auditions the first time. Hundreds of us in a huge room, and we waited hours. It was amazing. I can't wait to do my act for a really big audience. I hope the judges like my new jokes."

Josh's cheerfulness tugged at Luke's heart. He sat in his wheelchair, bent hands peeking out from under Luke's old leather jacket. He'd insisted on wearing it. Facing the world with courage and faith, the kid was way braver than he'd ever be.

A young woman in jeans and a *Talent Trek America* T-shirt dashed up to them, clipboard in hand. "Josh Harrison? I'm Sally, an assistant floor manager. Follow me. You too, Mom and Dad." She swiveled on one heel, dark pony tail swinging.

Luke hesitated. He hadn't planned on going on camera. This was the real thing, beamed live into millions of homes.

"Come on Dad!" Josh pulled at Luke's hand, tugging him towards the backstage area.

"I'll cheer you from the audience." Luke drew back, softening his refusal with a smile. "Your mom will be backstage with you."

"No." Josh's mouth set mulishly. "I want you both there. Like we're a real family."

Luke pressed his fingers to his eyes. He should have realized this would happen.

Could he risk being seen by someone from his past? If Anna found out about his criminal record the wrong way, he could kiss his hopes of them becoming a family goodbye. He had to tell her himself, and soon.

Tomorrow. He'd tell her tomorrow, once all this was over.

Even though that probably *still* meant kissing his hopes of a future together goodbye. Her dad taught her to judge any wrongdoing hard.

Maybe God would open her heart to hearing the truth. She'd softened toward him, since he'd told her about his new job. They'd felt like real partners as they'd cared for Josh and done things together.

He had to hope it would be enough. That knowing about the mistakes he'd made in the past wouldn't blind her to who he was now, thanks to God's grace.

"The producers want both parents backstage, if both are here," Sally said. "Move it."

His gaze met Anna's, over Josh's head. She smiled agreement, not just with her lips but with her eyes. Her face wore a sweetness that was almost a promise. "I'm okay with that."

A rising tide of hope surged in his chest. Maybe she'd be okay with the truth after all. Maybe she could forget her father's judgmental ideas, and accept and forgive instead. Maybe they really could be a family.

"Cowboy, you're on," he said, stepping forward to be the father Josh wanted him to be, on national TV.

Josh grinned his biggest grin, raising his arm for a high five.

Luke smiled as he returned the high five, but it worried him. Hardly any strength in the kid's slap. Despite his adrenaline-fueled perkiness, this trip was taking it out of him. They'd need to make sure he rested up well when they got home.

They followed Sally backstage, along a path cleared for Josh's chair through the chaotic tangle of cables and lights and cameras, and stood where she directed them to wait. She fitted his cordless microphone and tucked the transmitter box inside his jacket, but left it switched off.

"They're good," Josh whispered, nodding to the spectacular acrobats somersaulting and backflipping on stage. "Better than me. If I get to go on tour, I should take Pattie Pork Pie. I'm teaching her to do tricks."

"No Pattie." Anna's voice held a firmness that should warn Josh not to argue. "She wouldn't like all the noise and people. Way too stressful for her."

Josh argued anyway. "I'd win for sure if I had Pattie. Shouldn't I want to win?"

Luke chose his words carefully. "If you make people feel good and think about God as well, you'll win anyway, no matter what the vote is." He gently squeezed Josh's shoulder. "You're good too, cowboy. But comparing your act and the others is like asking which is better, apples or oranges."

Josh grinned. "Everyone from Sweetapple Falls knows the answer to that is pears! Maybe I can do what you said, and win too."

"I hope so. We'll be cheering you on."

Sally turned to shush them with an uplifted finger. The acrobats finished to a roar of applause from the audience and rave comments from the judges.

"You're up next, Josh," Sally said.

Luke fist bumped him, while Anna gave him a quick hug.

Sally bent to adjust Josh's microphone and switch it on. "You know the ropes by now. Break a leg!" She counted him in, then pointed for him to move into the spotlight.

Josh shifted his chair into gear and whirred onto the stage. Anna grabbed Luke's arm. All her attention was on Josh. Probably, she didn't even realize she'd taken hold of his arm. He covered her hand with his. Connection flowed between them, warm and comforting.

This was the way it should be. The way he hoped it could always be.

CHAPTER SIXTEEN

LUKE HELD HIS BREATH as Josh stopped his chair in the center of the stage. Whether the kid won or lost, Luke prayed he'd feel he succeeded tonight. Anna tensed beside him, her hand tightening on his arm.

The audience fell silent. Josh looked small and frail and fragile, alone in the bright lights. The huge brass gong used to dismiss rejected performers from the stage towered over him.

Please Lord, don't let him be gonged.

When they'd done this in rehearsal, crew sat in the judges' seats, and the empty arena echoed. Now, Josh faced world-famous judges, and a packed audience. Unfazed, he smiled at the judges, and waved at the crowd.

The judge Josh told him was known for her nastiness actually smiled back. "Tell us who you are, what your act is, and who's here with you tonight."

"I'm Josh Harrison, a middle school student from Sweetapple Falls, Oregon. Despite the name, my home town is famous for growing pears, not apples. I do sit-down comedy, and I hope I'll make you laugh tonight. I'm here with my Mom and Dad."

Sally pointed for Luke and Anna to look at the camera nearest them. They smiled and waved. His hand landed back over Anna's, still resting on his arm.

Her face creased in a little frown, as if finding her hand there surprised her. He lifted his hand so she could pull away if she wanted. Instead, she raised her eyes to his, seeming to search for something, some response from him. As his heart flipped over, he poured all he felt for her into his gaze.

Whatever she saw must have satisfied her. She gave a tiny smile and a nod, then focused on Josh again.

Luke could hardly breathe. In that nod, something shifted in their relationship. He watched Josh, but stayed achingly aware of Anna.

"How did you end up in a wheelchair?" asked another judge, a pretty brunette actress known for her tactless remarks.

"I've been doing comedy since I was a little kid. You know how before a performance everyone says break a leg? I heard it too many times, and ..." He waved his arms at his legs and the chair. "I guess no one ever said it to the guys before me."

The audience laughed.

Luke relaxed. Josh was on his way.

The rest of the act went without a hitch. A natural performer, the huge crowd and national television didn't affect Josh any more than getting up on the little stage at church. As he finished, with a wave of his cowboy hat, the audience erupted into cheers. From backstage, Luke and Anna clapped wildly too.

Face alight, Josh twisted to beckon them to join him. Sally nodded permission.

They stood either side of him, each with a hand on their son's shoulders. Josh swiveled his head to grin up at them then out at the applauding audience while the judges conferred. Luke's heart could burst with pride and joy.

The women judges gave enthusiastic remarks and voted yes.

Then the head judge commented, shaking his head. "I need talent who can tour the country in the final round. That's the only way through to the big prize. Good as your act is, I'm not sure you're up for it. You're too young, and your health might be an issue." He glanced at the judges flanking him. "The girls have never managed a tour. I have. I'm not voting you through."

Josh bowed his head. Disappointment for the boy flooded Luke, as tears gleamed in Anna's eyes. Taking any kid on tour would be complicated. Taking Josh would be a logistical nightmare.

But that hadn't stopped them hoping.

The thin shoulder beneath Luke's hand quivered. He silently prayed for his son.

Then Josh looked up and smiled at the audience. "Tour buses

aren't built for old Silver here." He patted his wheelchair. "But you guys get a say in who goes on tour, too."

Luke couldn't help grinning at Josh's bounce back. The kid's resilience amazed him.

The judge nodded, and spoke directly to camera. "He's right. It's up to the audience, here and at home. Your vote counts as much as ours tonight. So if you want to try to prove me wrong and let Josh go on tour, make sure you vote at the end of the show."

With one final wave, Josh maneuvered his chair offstage, Luke and Anna trailing behind him.

Sally put a finger to her lips for silence, and hustled them to the green room for their exit interview. Josh thanked God, Anna, and Luke in a performance rivaling an Academy Award acceptance speech.

Filming over, Sally patted Josh's back. "You were great. Good thing the Maestro was happy tonight. In the right mood, he loves it when talent talks back. In the wrong mood, forget it." She sliced a hand across her neck.

Luke smiled thanks. "We appreciate your help. I—"

A loud gong interrupted him, making them all jump and reverberating through the room.

"Oh no, Lamorna's been gonged." Sally frowned. "She won't be happy! I'll have to leave you now."

Josh burst into jubilant speech as the stage hand hurried away. "I hope I get voted through. I'm glad the Maestro didn't think I was too cheeky. Aren't you pleased you came on stage, Luke? We're just like a real family. Mom and Dad and me. That's what I want."

"That's what I want too."

Josh's face lit up even more. Something in Luke sang sweet as a skylark to see it. Like God's grace, he felt so undeserving of his son's love.

But it wasn't up to him, or Josh. That decision was Anna's. "When we get home, your mom and I need to talk things over and see what we can work out."

Luke met Anna's startled glance over Josh's head. He willed his eyes to tell her what his lips couldn't say right now. He wanted to ask her to marry him. And for more than Josh's sake. Because he loved her.

But before he told her how he felt, he had to tell her the truth. No more secrets.

And pray she'd understand.

Anna stared at Luke. There wasn't anything to work out. The only way he'd be moving in was if they were married, and he knew it.

But his warm dark eyes said things his words didn't. That he wanted them to be more than just Josh's Mom and Dad. Husband and wife, too. The same way he'd wanted to marry her, try to support them as a family, when she found she was expecting Josh.

She'd said no then, agreed with Dad they couldn't make it work.

If Luke asked her again, she'd give a different answer.

As the silent bonding between them lengthened and deepened, every cell in her body hummed with awareness of him. She held his gaze, not wanting to lose the effervescent joy bubbling through her. Luke seemed in no hurry to look away, either.

His eyes promised the safe haven she longed for. He'd proved himself, in so many ways, proved she could trust him to be a good father to their son. It wasn't much more of a step to trust him with her heart again. With every shallow breath she dragged into her lungs, with every second their gaze stayed connected, she inched closer to that step of faith, teetering right on the edge, ready to fall or fly.

Then the green room door slammed open, smashing into Josh's chair, snapping whatever stretched between them. She staggered, putting a hand onto Josh's chair to steady herself.

The petite teenaged singer who'd gone on stage after Josh burst through the open door, lovely face contorted, cursing like a sailor's parrot. She slammed her guitar against the wall, producing a discordant twang.

So Lamorna's sweet act was just that, an act.

"They gonged me. Me! I'm the favorite! I'm supposed to *win!*" The girl clutched her chest like a theatrical diva.

Josh pushed at his controls to move his chair back, but not fast enough for Lamorna.

"Out of my way, you jerk! They shouldn't let disabled kids on something like this. You'll never go on tour." She kicked at one wheel.

Anna tensed, clenching her fists. The pain of her nails digging into her palms reminded her to hold her temper. Lamorna was barely more than a child. Though if the girl did or said anything else to hurt Josh, she wouldn't hesitate to do whatever it took to stop her.

Lamorna stood scowling down at Josh, her chest heaving. Josh's eyes widened behind his glasses and his knuckles paled where he clutched his chair's controls. But he smiled, a charming, too-calm smile that spoke mischief.

No-one else smiled. Certainly not Luke. A vein pulsed in his forehead as he took a step forward.

Josh's jaw dropped in an assumed look of astonishment. He slapped his hand against the arm of his chair. "Wow! You're right, I *am* disabled. I never knew. Thank you so much for telling me." He smiled sweetly again, and pointed to the camera set up to record backstage tears and tantrums. "Aren't you glad this has all been filmed? When the video of this goes viral tomorrow, everyone will see how kind you were."

Lamorna's pink glossed lips curled. She raised her guitar and swung around as if to hit him, her long auburn hair and paisley 70s dress swirling around her.

Anna threw herself over Josh, braced for the guitar to smash against her. The blow never connected. Turning her head, she saw the guitar held safely in Luke's hands.

Lamorna glared at him, fingers curled like cat's claws. "I wouldn't have *really* hit him."

Anna wasn't so sure. She pushed herself upright, staying in front of Josh in case the girl struck out again.

Luke moved to shield them both. "It's too easy to threaten a kid in a wheelchair. Here, have this back. If you want to hit someone, try hitting me, instead."

Behind Luke's strength and solidity, Anna felt safe and protected. The breath she'd been holding whooshed out of her lungs and she collapsed against Josh's chair as her tense muscles relaxed. He'd make sure no-one hurt Josh. Or her.

Sally hurried over. "Security are on their way."

Defiance gone, Lamorna crumpled like a lost toddler. "No need. I won't cause any more trouble. I'm so sorry I did what I did."

"Where are your parents?" Luke asked, in a far gentler voice. "Don't you have someone with you?"

Shaking, she shook her head, tears starting in her eyes. "Dad probably headed straight for the bar when I got gonged. I'm supposed to make him rich. I won't now I'm out of the show, will I?" She covered her face with her hands, and cried, huge wrenching sobs.

A flash of pity for Lamorna surprised Anna. Losing a dream wasn't easy. As Sally put an arm around the distressed girl and led her away, Anna couldn't help praying for her.

Josh stared after Lamorna, pale but unhurt, a concerned crease between his brows.

"You okay?" Luke asked, putting one hand on Josh's shoulder and the other on her arm.

Reassurance, strength, and comfort flowed from his warm firm touch. When they needed him, he'd been there, for both of them. Her nod was shaky, but grateful. "Thank you. That could have gotten ugly. How about you, kiddo?"

Josh nodded too. "I'm fine. But I'm praying for her. It will get even worse for her tomorrow when what she did goes public." His slow thoughtful words sounded way older than his age.

How she'd managed to raise a kid so amazing and so mature, she didn't know. He certainly hadn't inherited it from her. She glanced at Luke, still feeling the warmth of his hand on her arm.

"I wanted to win, but I've decided I don't want it that badly," Josh said, shaking his head. "I'm okay if I don't go through to the tour. What happens next will be whatever God wants. I need to trust in Him." He nodded toward Lamorna, huddled sobbing across the room. "That's where not trusting and wanting the wrong things gets us."

Anna knew she didn't have a fraction of his faith.

Her son had more maturity at twelve than she had at thirty. She couldn't let go and forgive so easily, or accept everything that happened as God's will. She closed her eyes and dragged in a shaky breath.

In her heart, was her resistance to trusting Luke or God no more grown up than Lamorna? Like throwing an endless temper tantrum at God?

Pushing the prickly thought away, she looked for a distraction.

The catering crew set out fresh food for the contestants and their guests to graze while they waited for the public vote. The air hummed with adrenaline and nerves. Most of the contestants didn't look like they could eat a bite. Most of their guests weren't much better.

"Food?" she asked.

Josh suffered none of the other contestants' anxiety. He grinned. "Race you to the pizza!"

To her surprise, her stomach rumbled. She'd been so worried about Josh, she'd barely snacked all day. But if he was so relaxed about winning or losing, she could relax too. Five minutes later they sat at a small round table, a pizza between them.

Luke reached for a slice. "Josh, your goal with winning is to get your own TV show, right?"

Josh nodded, chewing slowly.

"So why not start your own Internet TV channel?" Luke raised his eyebrows, grinning like a kid.

Anna bit her lip. She wanted Josh to have everything he wanted, but even with Luke's help these trips emptied their bank account. They couldn't afford expensive equipment.

"I've been reading up on it," Luke continued. "You have a good enough computer, and we can probably borrow most of what you'll need."

Anna loosed the breath she'd been holding. She wouldn't have to say no.

Josh's face lit up as if a light switched on. "You betcha! Will you help me?"

"Sure. You have a deal, cowboy." Luke offered Josh his hand to shake.

Josh started in on enthusiastic plans. They got so technical they could have been talking Greek, for all she understood. But hearing Josh so excited made Anna happy, too.

When Luke first came back, she would have been jealous. Felt excluded by their boy talk, the two dark heads so close together, the arms that waved in similar gestures as they spoke. Now, she could see Luke was exactly what Josh needed.

As if he sensed her eyes on him, Luke smiled across the table at her. A slow deep smile full of promise.

Something hard and solid in her chest melted in the warmth. He flickered a wink, then turned back to Josh. It was enough. He wasn't only what Josh needed. She needed him, too.

They sat there until the performers were called on stage for the announcement of tonight's winners. Parents were asked to accompany anyone under sixteen. Anna soon realized why.

Designed to maximize stress, dazzling spotlights blinded the contestants while thumping music shook and deafened them. One by one, the MC called the names of the eliminated contestants, and their spotlights dimmed. He dragged it out as far as he could, delaying each announcement.

At last, only three pools of light remained. Josh, the acrobats, and a magician. She clutched Josh's shoulder, heart throbbing in time with the music.

"Three acts remain on stage," the MC intoned. "Only two will go through to the national tour. One will leave, their hopes shattered forever. And the acts through to the tour, as voted by the judges and you the public ..."

They waited. And waited. And waited.

Her pulse pounded in her ears, louder than the drumbeats. Though he'd said he didn't care, Josh's shoulder quivered beneath her hand.

Just when she thought she'd faint from the suspense, the MC shouted, "Josh, and Acrobatsia!"

He'd made it! Relief flooded her, as the theater erupted into applause.

She and Luke bent to hug an ecstatic Josh. Impulsively, she hugged Luke too. With her arms wrapped around him, she lifted her head to meet his eyes and saw the joy she felt mirrored there.

And something more. An honesty and depth of feeling that caught the breath in her throat. Without thinking, she reached up, grabbed his face, and kissed him.

Their lips met and clung. His arms tightened around her, warming her all the way through with tenderness and caring. For a long moment she didn't want to end, his sweet gentle kiss carried her to a place where all that mattered was the two of them. Luke's lips spoke a wordless message of hope.

Then slowly and gently, he pulled back.

She didn't want to let him go. But this wasn't the time or the place for kisses.

That would come.

She'd tried to stop herself trusting or needing Luke, but it was too late. If Luke asked her to marry him, she knew what her answer would be. Gladly, joyfully, she'd say yes. Not just for Josh's sake, but for her own. She couldn't pretend any longer, couldn't ignore the truth.

She loved Luke.

She'd never stopped loving him, and she never would.

CHAPTER SEVENTEEN

ANNA SANG AS SHE WASHED the breakfast dishes on Monday morning.

Her life held so many blessings. Sunshine streamed into her kitchen. Maggie left a message, saying another painting sold on Saturday. Josh buzzed with joy over *Talent Trek*.

And Luke? Well, maybe he was something to sing about, too.

The weekend had gone crazy. The video of Lamorna's outburst went viral, as Josh predicted. He'd done interview after interview on Sunday and looked set to be the new poster boy for disabled rights.

She'd been glad of Luke's support through it all. Thinking of him warmed her all over. His help with Josh made things so much easier.

And it wasn't just how he was with Josh that sweetened her life. She'd spent hours in Luke's company every day for weeks. They'd seen more of each other since his return than many couples who'd dated six months or longer. She'd seen enough to recognize the man he'd become. And to risk trusting him with her heart again.

Though he'd looked oddly serious when he'd taken Josh to school this morning.

Asked if they could talk when he got back.

On Saturday night, he'd hinted...

The dishcloth dropped, and her hands rose to cover her mouth. The breath stopped in her chest. Was he planning to propose this morning?

She burst out laughing as the wonder of the idea spread though her like a flower blooming. She glanced up at the clock, then down at her old housework clothes. Twenty-five minutes before he got back.

"Pattie girl," she said to the piglet dozing in her basket in the corner, "I think I'd better go make myself a bit prettier, just in case."

Upstairs in her bedroom, she put on a favorite dress and slipped her feet into her nicest flats. Started doing something with her hair. Then the front door bell interrupted her.

It couldn't be Luke yet. A peek out the window showed the deputy's car. Her eyes rolled at Connor's bad timing. Still, she could deal with whatever he wanted and get rid of him fast enough.

But when she opened the door, Connor's somber expression reminded her of the day he'd told her Mom and Dad had died. He'd used the front door then, too. Her heart stopped beating then galloped. His face wavered before her eyes.

"Josh? Is he okay? Or is it Luke?" She forced words from her tight lungs.

"No immediate emergency." Connor's stern expression offered no reassurance. "But I have information you need to be aware of. May I come in?"

Forcing her shaky legs to move, she led him into the living room, and sat on the couch. "What information?"

Connor stood stiffly. "I didn't like the way Luke Tanner appeared out of nowhere. Too like those stalkers after Josh did *Talent Trek* the first time. I made inquiries into his background." He placed a large envelope on the low table in front of her. "Seeing him on TV triggered a cop buddy's memory. He sent me this. You need to know who you're letting into your home and allowing your son to associate with."

Her singing joy evaporated faster than morning dew in summer. She made no move to pick up the envelope, knowing she wouldn't like what it contained.

She'd lost too much, she couldn't lose what was growing between her and Luke too, just when she'd started to let herself hope.

Connor pushed it towards her. "You need to read this, Anna. Your father never liked him, you know that. Ignoring the facts won't make them go away."

Anger prickled her. She shook her head. "I can see who Luke is now. That's enough for me."

His lips thinned. "People don't change, Anna. They're good, or they're bad. Your father taught me that. He knew the boy who got you into trouble was one of the bad ones. But you couldn't see it. What makes you think your judgment's any better now?"

Surely Luke had proved himself. People *could* change. Couldn't they?

She bit her lip and looked up at Connor. His clear gaze shone with concern and conviction.

Like a little girl praying if she doesn't look, the monster will vanish, she closed her eyes. Maybe ignoring the facts would make them go away.

"Your father was a good lawman, and a good judge of character. Luke Tanner isn't who you think he is." Connor's firm voice rang with certainty. "This isn't anything personal. It's me doing my job."

Doubt seeped into her, a killing frost shriveling the fragile trust she'd felt. Dad had trusted Connor. Hoped she'd marry his deputy, till she came home pregnant and shamed.

After that, Connor married Suzy instead.

She clasped her hands together to stop them trembling. Her hopes of a life with Luke crashed down around her again. "Does your information suggest I shouldn't leave him alone with Josh?"

Connor's lips tightened. "Read those reports, and make up your own mind." Then he shook his head. "I don't believe he'd endanger Josh, no." The reluctant words seemed dragged from him.

Relief surged through Anna. Connor always told the truth.

No matter how much she cared for Luke and no matter that she couldn't believe he'd hurt Josh, keeping her son safe was her biggest priority.

"Your father would have wanted me to tell you straight." Connor turned his deputy's hat in his hands, the way she'd seen her father do so many times. "If your father's memory means anything to you, you'll end it with Tanner, now." He stood straight and tall, in his khaki deputy's uniform, the same uniform her father had been so proud to wear.

She glanced at Dad's photo, framed on the wall along with his badge. All her life she'd tried to be a good girl, do what he wanted her to do. Only once had she gone against him, and he never forgave her that.

Was she betraying him all over again by trusting Luke?

Her heart wasn't just breaking. It was smashed. Shattered. Pulverized into so many pieces she'd never put them back together again.

Needing to sound a whole lot calmer than she felt, she dragged in a deep breath. "Thank you, Connor." She picked up the envelope. "I'll read what's in here. Do you mind leaving now?"

He rested a hand on her arm, intended to comfort, but she felt nothing but coldness, all the way through.

The Deputy's hard voice gentled, "Anna, I'm not saying this to hurt you. You know I hoped we'd be more than friends. I only want the best for you. Luke Tanner isn't that."

Her hands convulsed in her lap. She knew Connor was a good man. One of the best, just like her dad. But not the man for her. "I'm sorry. It's only ever been Luke for me. No matter whether he stays or goes, no matter what's in those reports you brought, that's not changing."

He nodded slowly. "So what are you going to do?"

"I don't know. I'll read this, and pray." Somehow, she managed to stand and put one foot in front of the other to show him out.

She closed the door behind him, and sat at the kitchen table turning the envelope over in her hands. Fingers shaking, sick to her stomach, she muttered a quick prayer and opened it. After reading the brutally stark reports, she wanted to run to the bathroom to throw up.

Connor and Dad were right. Luke wasn't who she'd thought he was. She really couldn't trust her own judgment.

If even half those reports were true, Luke had lied to her. Not just in the past, but now, too. She'd made a huge mistake, letting Josh be with him, softening to him, opening her heart to him again.

Luke Tanner wasn't the man she'd thought.

Instead, he was a convicted criminal. The sort Dad locked up and despised. She shouldn't have trusted him at seventeen, and she shouldn't have trusted him now. Dad had been right to stop her making the biggest mistake of her life by marrying Luke.

And now she'd been saved from making that same mistake again. Luke couldn't possibly love her, if he'd hidden all this.

Knowing that shouldn't make her feel so sick.

Luke turned the van down Anna's street, and the deputy's vehicle passed him. Connor looked straight through him, as if he didn't exist.

Foreboding shivered Luke. He'd left it too late to tell Anna the truth. Connor got there first.

The media frenzy after *Talent Trek* made it more likely his past would come out, but he'd hoped it wouldn't happen this soon. He should have known better.

His hands tightened on the steering wheel until his fingers numbed. Anna wouldn't forgive him. Her trust in him was too new and too fragile. The best he could hope was that she'd let him see Josh now and then.

He parked the van in the drive, in its usual place. He walked up to the back door to give the keys back to Anna, the way he usually did. But there was nothing usual about the way he felt as he knocked on the door. Legs heavy and reluctant, he knew he'd walk into a kangaroo court where Anna was judge, jury, and executioner.

Forcing out a tight breath, he tried to believe Connor visited for something else. But he couldn't kid himself. Anna knew.

She opened the door, and her closed and distant expression, bleak as mid-winter, doused the hope sparking in his heart as surely as a bucket of cold water. Arms crossed tightly over her chest, she stood in the doorway, denying him entry. Just like the first time he'd knocked on her door.

"Luke." The single word fell heavy between them.

An icy ball of dread settled in his chest, and he dragged a breath into lungs that seemed to have frozen solid. "You agreed before I left we could talk. May I come in?"

She shook her head. "I'm not sure I can talk now. I need time by myself, to think things through."

Holding a hand out toward her, he prayed that somehow he could reach her. "Anna, I don't know what Connor told you, but I'd planned to explain about my past today."

No surprise, she ignored his outstretched hand. "Why, so you could put your spin on it and charm me with more lies?" Her tone held sadness than anger.

"I haven't lied to you since I came back, and I won't. Not to you, and not to Josh."

"But you lied to me in the past. And you haven't told me the truth since you returned." She squeezed her eyes shut for a moment. "Would you believe I was actually hoping you planned to propose?

Look, I got dressed up for you." Hands dropping to her sides, she pulled at the skirt of her pretty blue dress.

"Anna —"

She interrupted, shaking her head. "How could I have been such a fool? My father was right about you." Her body folded in on itself. "How can I believe anything else you say? Why didn't you tell me?" The words emerged almost as a wail.

Her distress wrapped round his chest like a giant fist and squeezed tight. He longed to hold her, to take that pain away. But he'd caused it. While he hesitated, she straightened, retreating behind her protective wall again.

Gulping for breath, he tried to meet her eyes. Explanations seemed pointless, but he had to try. What they had was too important to give up on.

"I've known for weeks I had to tell you. I was waiting for the right time." He shook his head at his stupidity. "And yes, I did plan to ask you to marry me. But not until after you knew. If only she'd listen, maybe he could change her mind. "Please, let me in so we can talk about this."

She studied him, eyes narrowed and distrustful, then stood back to allow him into the kitchen.

Scattered sheets of paper lay on the table, on top of a large manila envelope.

Anna nodded at them. "That's what Connor brought me." She sat on the straight backed wooden chair near the window, drawing her knees up under her full skirt and hugging them. "It can't be explained away, Luke. It's too much."

Despite her defensiveness, something about her looked so small and lost that he wanted to wrap his arms around her. But he'd missed his chance.

He didn't give more than a glance to the papers, grainy scans of old faxes and police reports. He could guess what they held. Nothing good.

"That is my past." He nodded at the pile of papers, then thumped a fist on his chest. "This is me. God has made me more since then."

Her arms tightened around her legs, and her face scrunched. "I don't know who you are, any more. It's like one minute I stood on solid ground, then a great wave washed me flat. Now I'm in deep water way over my head. Please. Tell me the truth. Those reports say horrible things."

He collected the papers, and sat in the chair opposite her. No more than the kitchen table separated them physically, but Anna felt so far away, it could have been a mile wide.

Swallowing hard, he read the first page. Only the tightness of every muscle in his body stopped his hands from shaking.

A Social Services report, from before Mom's frequent moves let them fall through the cracks in the system. His first twelve years of life, reduced to a few sentences describing her parenting as erratic and inadequate. That was about right. But she'd tried for a while.

A string of dates showed when he'd been taken away, into children's homes or foster care, and when he'd been given back to her. Like a package no one really wanted or knew what to do with.

The second page was the police report on her death.

A grainy photo showed her on their apartment floor, bruised and battered from her boyfriend's beatings. The way he'd last seen her. Seeing it again in black and white clenched his heart in a vice grip.

Seeing himself listed as a potential suspect made it even worse.

Grief and regret and guilt swelled upwards, closing off his throat. The pages in front of him blurred, and dropped into his lap, as his hands formed fists and lifted to cover his mouth. He pressed his lips against his teeth, welcoming the pain.

Easier to feel the pain than deal with the evidence of how badly he'd failed her.

He'd been a kid. It wasn't his job to save his mom. But he'd felt like it was. If only she'd loved him enough, or if only he'd taken better care of her, surely she wouldn't have chosen to go back to the drugs and the drink every single time. If only he'd been able to stop her.

But she'd loved the drugs more than she loved him.

His chest heaved with the silent sobs he hadn't been able to loose when she'd died. He couldn't release them now, either.

Not with Anna sitting there in silent judgment. He didn't dare glance at her, risk seeing her reaction to his weakness. With an effort, he forced the feelings down, rubbing his eyes with his fists so he could see enough to read. The report contained nothing but the facts, stark and brutal. No feeling for the loss of a human life, no sense this person meant anything.

His fingers clenched on the edges of the page as he tried and failed to read the impersonal words as they referred to a stranger.

He closed his eyes. The words cut, like walking barefoot on broken glass. Each one lacerated closer to the bone than the last. His love hadn't been enough to stop his mom destroying herself.

Anna sat pulled into that same tight closed-off ball. Her only move had been to lay her head on her knees and close her eyes as if she was tired.

He was tired too. Tired of carrying the heavy load of guilt at failing Mom. Tired of the certainty that when anyone knew the truth, they'd reject him, the way Mom had.

Now it was happening all over again, Anna's second rejection cut even deeper than Mom's had.

CHAPTER EIGHTEEN

ANNA DIDN'T KNOW HOW to respond to Luke.

Her arms clenched tighter around her knees. Anything to stop herself reaching out to him. To see him hunched over the table and so distraught tortured her.

But she had to stay strong, remind herself she couldn't judge character. Her feelings for Luke turned out to be as untrustworthy as the man himself. Everything in the reports told her Luke wasn't the man she'd thought.

She should throw him out the house.

Instead, his grief for his mom made her chest ache, reminding her how she'd felt when Mom and Dad died. She longed to wrap her arms around him, hold him as he cried out his loss, the way she'd longed for someone to hold her.

But she couldn't risk getting close to Luke again. It wasn't just his childhood and his mom. The reports hit her with sledgehammer force, smashing her trust in him. He was a liar and a thief, a convicted criminal, a stranger to her.

He couldn't possibly love her, if he'd lied to her about so much.

Shuttering her expression, she handed him a box of tissues, and sat still and silent while he got himself back under control.

He blew his nose, then started talking, his voice so low she had to lean closer to hear. "If you only believe one thing about me, believe I didn't hurt my mom." His fists knotted and unknotted on the table. "I know I made it sound like I'd grown up in a much better home than I did. The truth was, I never had a real home. I was in and out of foster care because Mom couldn't look after me. I tried to stop her using drugs and drinking. I tried to stop her boyfriend beating her."

"Her boyfriend?" Anna's hand rose to cover her mouth. She'd seen the bruises on his mom's photo. The report stated that the teenage son was a suspected perpetrator, but she couldn't believe that of Luke.

His lips twisted in a humorless smile. "Some boyfriend. He brought her drugs, took her money, and beat her. The night she died, I finally stopped him. He broke my nose, but I made him leave her alone. At fifteen, I was big enough to protect her. I felt like the champion of the world."

He rubbed the bump on his nose. Now she knew why he did that so often. The horror of it burned her tight lungs. Only a few years older than Josh, and he'd lived like that.

Luke's gaze lifted to hers, but she looked away, not daring to let him see how his past affected her. She had to keep that door closed tight, remember he hadn't trusted her enough to tell the truth.

Everything he'd told her when they first met was a lie. She didn't know him anymore.

He loosed a sigh, then continued talking. "I thought she'd be pleased. Nope. She was angry. She'd have to go find drugs somewhere else. I begged her to stay home, but her addiction ran her life. I didn't see her alive again."

Anna didn't speak. There were no words. Nothing she could say would make this better.

"Normally I woke when she came in, and made sure she was okay. That night, I didn't hear her come home. In the morning, I found her like this." Grimacing, he pointed at the police report of her death. His throat moved as he swallowed hard.

The struggle to control himself played out on his face. It was a long time before he spoke again. "It wasn't the first time she'd passed out on the floor. But this time was different. Her color was wrong. Her skin was cold. She didn't respond."

Acid burned in her chest at the thought of the boy he'd been facing that. She pressed her hands against her mouth.

Shame clouded Luke's desolate eyes and he seemed to crumple. "I didn't know what to do. Mom always said to avoid the police or the authorities. So I threw some clothes and our personal papers into a grocery sack, and ran. I called the ambulance from a payphone. When they brought her out on a covered gurney, I knew I was on my own."

Anna struggled to imagine how that must have felt. Her parents dying hit her hard, but she'd had a secure home and Josh to live for. Luke was fifteen, homeless, and alone. She clamped her heart down tight on the anguish of that thought.

It only proved it was safer not to love and trust. Everyone died or left you. And God was the least trustworthy of all. He let terrible things like this happen.

To her. To Josh. To Luke.

She guessed he'd never spoken to anyone about this before. Like pressure opening a crack in a dam wall wider and wider until the whole thing collapsed, words poured out of him.

"I'd found a building site I could sneak into at night, and left a couple of old blankets hidden there. Somewhere to go when Mom brought men back to the apartment. I didn't want to leave her, but I couldn't bear to be around sometimes."

He shook his head, as if shaking memories loose.

"One day, I slept late. The foreman of the building team found me. I thought he'd call the cops or boot me out. Instead, he offered me a job laboring for the team in the day, and let me stay there at night. He probably guessed I was underage and he could get away with paying me less than minimum wage. When they moved to their next job they kept me on. I found a cheap shared room I could sleep in. Things were okay for a few years."

He looked up and straight at her. "Then I met you."

His simple recital left Anna broken and wide open to Luke. He'd lived through so much, far more than anyone should have to.

But this man was a stranger to her. He'd lied to her. He'd betrayed her trust. Chances were, he'd leave her and Josh all over again.

She had to be strong.

While Luke talked, he'd wanted only to get the truth out. It hadn't mattered what Anna thought. Now though, it mattered. She stared at him, sorrow, compassion, and mistrust battling it out in her eyes.

Mistrust won.

Brick by brick, she rebuilt the wall between them. He saw it, in her blanked expression and shuttered eyes.

The first time he'd been taken into care, his foster mom locked him in a cupboard and left him there all day, though he banged on the door till his hands hurt. The sense of helplessness and rejection now was the same.

"Anna?" He reached across the table.

Biting her lip, she shook her head. "I believe you about your mom. No kid should have to suffer like that. I hate thinking you went through what you did. But you lied when I asked about your family."

He looked away, shifting uncomfortably in his seat. "You were everything I'd never dared dream of. Beautiful. Smart. Talented. From a nice home in a nice town. You had a deputy for a dad and a mom who baked you cookies. I slept six to a room in a house only one step better than sleeping on the streets, my mom never baked a cookie in her life, and I'm not sure she knew who my father was. How could I tell you the truth?"

Anna rubbed her hands over her face. "How could you *not* tell me the truth?"

He could barely speak past the thickness in his throat. "I tried not to talk about my background. I didn't want to lie."

Her lips tightened. "You did lie. And there are other reports. If it was just your mom, I could forgive you. But you've kept so much from me."

His belly knotted as he picked up the next page. Repeated thefts of money and liquor from a Eugene convenience store. Enough to add up to a Class C felony, punishable by five years incarceration.

The suspect — a former worker at the store. Luke Tanner. The Kolinskys filed the report a week after he left the country with House the World, exactly as Stan told him they would. His only good foster parents practiced tough love, but it was real love, too.

"Is it true?" Ice edged Anna's voice. "Did you steal all that?"

His gaze stayed fixed on the table. He knew her opinion of thieves, no need to see it chilling her eyes.

Remorse at the way he'd betrayed the only people who'd really cared for him clamped a tight fist round his heart. The Kolinskys had given him a chance. He'd repaid their kindness by stealing from them. He closed his eyes and scrubbed at his aching chest with one hand as if he could erase the guilt.

Somehow, he dragged enough air past the blockage in his throat to speak. "Yes. When I met you, I earned enough to support myself.

After you'd gone home expecting Josh, I still hoped you'd marry me, so I tried hard to earn enough to support a family. The Kolinskys gave me evening work in their store."

Shame at his inability to provide like a man should burned in his belly. He hadn't been a man.

Just a kid trying his best to be one.

Anna said nothing, so he continued, low voiced.

"After you signed the adoption papers and said you wouldn't marry me, I went a little crazy." He held up his hands before she could protest. "Not blaming you. You were right. But it was a kick in the guts to be rejected after I'd tried so hard. With nothing to work toward or hope for anymore, I stopped trying. Started doing drink and drugs to numb the pain. Then I stole to pay for it."

Her chair creaked. She lowered her legs and leaned forward. The intense disappointment on her face lacerated him. "I'm sorry for your pain. Truly, I am. But finding all this out now makes me feel I've been trusting a stranger."

He jumped up and paced the room, unable to keep still any longer under that painful gaze. "My past isn't who I am now. I'm still the same man you thought I was yesterday."

She shook her head. Emotion paled her cheeks and clenched her fists. "No. You're not. You thought I'd rejected you? Well, I felt rejected too, when you just disappeared. Like all you cared about was the baby, and once I said he could be adopted, you didn't want me. But I didn't go crazy and break the law. I had a sick baby to look after. By the time he was three months old and had a diagnosis, you were long gone."

"I'm not making excuses." Her set face showed his protests were pointless, but he had to try. "I know what I did was wrong. Thankfully, I got busted. I'm sure you saw the other reports too, for possession of narcotics. I could have gone to jail, but my foster parents cut a deal with the judge. Community service with House the World instead. The Kolinskys knew about the stealing, but didn't file the report till after I left, I guess to make sure I knew what was waiting for me if I ran away from the mission."

Anna didn't respond.

So this was it. Frozen out forever.

He stopped his restless pacing. Hands gripping the back of the sofa, he swallowed, and raised his eyes to Anna. "I hoped once you knew, you could accept my past. See who I am now, not who I was."

"I can't." Her voice shook with emotion. "How can I trust you? How do I know you won't do it again when things get tough with Josh? How can I believe you're telling the truth about anything, when you lied about this?"

"Anna—"

She interrupted him with a chopping wave of her hands.

"I wish I could tell you to leave and never come back. But that would hurt Josh. You can still see him. But there's no chance now of anything between us. You and I…"

Her voice trailed off as pain creased her face. She closed her eyes and swiped her hands across them.

It was as if the weeks since he arrived here hadn't happened. Everything he'd done to win her trust — gone. He'd thought his mother dying had been painful. He'd thought leaving Anna and Josh behind in the hospital had been painful.

Nope. Not like this. He hadn't truly let himself hope for better before. This time, he had. He'd believed God wanted them to be a family.

But he knew Anna. She wouldn't change her mind. Her father taught her too well. They'd never be a family now.

Anna straightened, making her spine as stiff and inflexible as the hard chair. Maybe at last, she could be the girl her father loved and approved of again. Make up for her wrong choices over Luke last time.

Luke, who'd proved twice over that he didn't really love her.

"I'm Josh's mother, you're Josh's father. That's all there is between us, and all there can ever be."

Luke couldn't get the wrong idea or hope she'd change her mind. If he'd forget about her and just see Josh, things would be so much easier. She rubbed suddenly chilled hands together as loss shivered through her.

This was what she wanted, wasn't it?

"We'll work out a schedule. You can take Josh to Power Soccer on Saturdays. If you tell me when you'll be helping him with his video stuff, I'll make sure I'm out. And you can see him at Scouts on

Wednesdays. We won't need to meet." Her voice sounded oddly distant in her ears. "You'll be working in Orchard Bridge, so it might be better if you lived and worshiped there too."

She couldn't tell Luke that the real reason she didn't want to see him was the fear coiling in her belly, fear her resolve would weaken around him. She couldn't take the risk of loving Luke. She just couldn't.

But Josh wanted a father, and she wouldn't take that away from him.

Luke paced to the fireplace, gripping the mantelpiece in one strong hand. She forced down the memory of the feel of that hand, warm on hers. Or cradling her face as he kissed her. Thoughts like that only made her weak.

"Josh wants me putting him to bed and getting him up. How do we handle that?"

Her trembling hands clenched into fists as she jumped up from her chair. "Josh was happy with me doing that for him before you came along. He'll have to accept he needs his mom to do some things for him, no matter how much he wants to live in your boys-only world."

Luke eyed her. "That sounds like you're jealous."

Anna refused to feel shame, though she couldn't stop her cheeks heating. "Of course I'm jealous. I raised him alone for all these years. Then you come back, and do the father-son stuff. You take him skiing. You fix the car and paint the house and make videos. So he wants you, not me." Pain shook her, and she took a deep breath to force it down. "And now I find out you lied all along. You weren't around when we needed you, because you broke the law and had to run. How am I supposed to feel?"

He raised his chin, and his lips tightened. "I've worked hard since then. I paid back every penny I stole. I haven't touched drugs or drink for years. Doesn't that mean anything? I let you down once, but never again."

His words vibrated with such passion he tempted her to believe him, to trust him, but she knew she had to hold to her resolve. She couldn't trust herself and she couldn't trust Luke.

"This isn't about me being jealous of you and Josh. It's not really about you stealing or using drugs, either. It's a trust thing. We're back at square one, Luke." She strengthened her voice to stop it shaking.

"Leave town for a few days. When you come back, text me and I'll make arrangements for you to see Josh. I'd rather we didn't meet, unless we have to."

Hoping her bravado lasted till he left, she marched to the door and flung it open.

"You won't tell Josh…" He gestured at the papers.

The struggle to contain her fury forced a long hissing breath between her clenched teeth.

She turned back, shoved the reports in the envelope and whacked him in the chest with it. "Of course I won't tell Josh. That you'd even ask proves you don't know me at all."

Luke opened his mouth, looked for a moment like he'd argue. A muscle pulsed in his jaw. Then he took the papers and walked to the door, turning back to her at the threshold. "I'm sorry it's ending like this."

Sadness flooded Anna, but she refused to let it show on her face. "I am too. Please, go now."

He stepped through the door.

The moment she closed the door behind him, she collapsed against it. All her strength oozed away.

She couldn't hurt Josh by taking his dad away from him, but she could take back her heart. She could get her life organized, in neat manageable compartments. Luke had his son. Josh had his dad. She had her life back, and Luke needn't be a part of it.

Everyone had what they wanted and could be happy.

So why did she feel empty as a hollowed out Halloween pumpkin?

Once she heard Luke's truck drive away, she straightened the chairs they'd been sitting in and planned her day.

Paintings in the studio to complete.

Making space for Josh to set up his TV studio.

And there were always cookies to be baked.

Something in her told her she should pray, but she didn't want to risk God telling her she'd made a mistake. This was the right thing. It had to be.

When her cellphone rang, she considered ignoring it. Probably Luke. Then she saw the caller display.

Josh's school.

Her heart pounded as she snatched up the phone. For regular messages, they rang the house number. The cell number was for emergencies.

They'd only call it if something was wrong.

Very wrong.

CHAPTER NINETEEN

LUKE GOT AS FAR AS the next street before he had to pull over. Tears blurred his eyes too much to drive, and he couldn't risk causing an accident. He turned off the engine and buried his head in his hands.

He'd arrived in Sweetapple Falls angry with Anna, wanting to be part of his son's life, not hers. God gave him exactly what he asked for.

It should be enough, but it wasn't.

Despair washed over him like a tidal wave, as he slumped behind the steering wheel.

Lord, help me, show me the way.

Words from Dan's last sermon popped into his mind. "We can only love others as much as we love ourselves."

He couldn't love himself. The reasons sat beside him in that envelope on the passenger seat. Did his lack of self-love and self-respect mean he couldn't love Anna the way she needed? Was that why she doubted him so easily, why she knew she couldn't trust him?

A long breath escaped him at his unanswerable questions.

He rubbed his eyes, and started the truck. Anna wanted him to leave town for a few days. He would. The police report made him realize he hadn't made full recompense to Stan and Beth, his foster parents.

Sure, he'd repaid the money, but sending checks was easy. He'd never done the hard part of righting a wrong. He'd never admitted his offense, asked their forgiveness, or thanked them for sending him to House the World.

The kid he'd been, barely able to read or write and working menial jobs hadn't been a fit husband for Anna or a fit father for Josh. That kid never could have cared for them right, back then.

If God had a plan, then this was all part of it.

Slowly, he drove to the church house. Dan looked up as Luke passed his office, and followed him to his room.

"Luke! I missed touching base with you last night. I hoped we'd talk today." Dan's broad smile made the worst possible match for how Luke felt.

He'd expected Dan would ask him to leave, now his work was done. "No need to ask me to go. I'll be away for a couple of days, then I'll make arrangements to move."

"Oh great! You're marrying Anna? You guys seemed pretty friendly on TV." The genuine joy in his friend's voice tortured Luke.

He shook his head. "You know what they say, don't trust everything you see on TV."

"What's wrong?"

Luke gestured for Dan to sit down. "I made some mistakes in the past, and got in trouble with the law. Anna found out from someone else. And I lied to her when we first met. All long before I became a Christian." He looked away. The memories burned too much to talk about yet. "I'll tell you another time. Upshot is, she feels she can't trust me."

Simple words to describe a life in pieces, once again.

Dan didn't interrupt, just looked at him with that calm accepting gaze that made him such a good pastor.

Luke loosed another long breath. "No chance of her marrying me. I'm grateful she'll still let me see Josh." His shoulders sagged and he closed his eyes. He tried to pray, but his words seemed to hit the ceiling and bounce back at him.

"What are you going to do?" Dan showed no sign of judging him.

No need. Luke was already judging himself, and Anna's opinion looked merciful in comparison. "She wants me gone for a few days. I'll go see my old foster parents in Eugene, put things right with them."

Dan nodded. "You don't need to move out. Stay here for as long as you need."

"There's a bathroom and kitchenette at the new office in Orchard

Bridge. I'll set things up to sleep there."

"That's not exactly a home."

"It will do." Luke's lips twisted in a humorless smile. He pulled his overnight bag out of the wardrobe. Packing took all of thirty seconds. Moving out wouldn't be hard. Everything he owned still fit into one suitcase.

His whole childhood had been like that. He'd lost count how many times they'd moved. Why, he'd never known. All he knew was that they were moving, again.

"I'll pray for you." Dan enveloped him in a bear hug.

The comfort of it surprised Luke. Was this what a hug from a brother or a father felt like? He thumped Dan's back. "I appreciate your faith in me. I'll make sure I'm back for Wednesday night Scouts with Josh. I'll text him to let him know that."

"God works in ways that are beyond us." Dan gave him a hopeful smile. "Anna might change her mind."

Luke shook his head. "I'm not wasting time hoping for that. I can still see Josh, that's what counts. And I can serve God through House the World. He doesn't plan marriage for all of us."

"I know. But I couldn't help feeling…" Dan stopped, seeming to reconsider his overly optimistic words. "Travel safely. You'll have a place here when you come back."

"Thanks." Luke picked up his bag and walked to the door. A thought hit him, sickening him like a kick to his belly. He turned back.

"See that envelope on the table?"

Dan picked it up. "This?"

Luke nodded, mouth dry. "It's the reports Connor dug up." He bit his lip and shook his head. "If he found them, other people can, too. After this weekend's publicity, it could get into the newspapers. I don't want Josh finding out that way. I asked Anna not to tell him, but now I think he needs to know. Will you…?"

He trailed off. Asking Dan to do his dirty work felt wrong, but he couldn't bear to see the respect in Josh's eyes fade.

"Of course." Dan's eyes creased in concern. "Are you sure you're okay?"

Luke shrugged. "I have to be."

Three hour's drive up the I-5 S later, he stood outside a blue painted door in a quiet Eugene street. He'd been ten years old and terrified, the first time he'd seen this door.

After his previous foster carers, he'd expected the worst.

Their neat clapboarded houses looked similar on the outside. They'd smiled just as nicely in front of the social workers. But those facades hid abuse that made life with Mom look good. Twitching his hand out of Stan's grasp, he'd run as fast as he could.

Thankfully, Stan ran faster. Luke soon found the Kolinskys were different from his other foster parents.

He wouldn't try to run this time, though he didn't know how they'd receive him. But he wanted to show he'd truly repented. Whispering a prayer to settle the nerves twitching his stomach, he took a deep breath, and knocked.

He recognized Beth as soon as she opened the door. At seventy, silver threaded her dark hair, and her face bore more creases.

She broke into a welcoming smile. "Luke! I hoped you'd visit!" Her arms opened wide, inviting a hug.

He swept her into his arms. Emotion tightened his chest. He didn't deserve this welcome, but Beth showed nothing but delight to see him. He'd never realized how tiny she was, barely up to his chest. But Beth and Stan were big in spirit. Being in her presence again humbled him.

She returned his hug with vigor, then stood back, staring up at him. "You've grown."

He smiled. "It's been twelve years. I hope I've grown in more ways than up. I'm a believer now."

"Thank God," she said simply, and grinned. "Sit down. I'll call Stan in. He gave up the store last year, and is making up for lost time in the yard."

She led him into the compact living room. Nothing had changed, just faded and worn a little more. The same checked fabric on the 80's couch. The same framed print of Jesus on the wall, gazing into the room with serene compassion.

He stood waiting for Stan, holding his breath as the solid man who was the closest thing he'd had to a father hurried into the room.

"Luke! Good to see you, son." The words warmed Luke as much as his old foster father's beaming smile and hearty handshake. Stan's grasp was as firm as ever. He sat, waving Luke into a seat.

Beth bustled in with a tray of coffee and ciasteczka, the sweet Polish cookies she'd only allowed as a rare treat. "Isn't this a special occasion, when a son comes home?"

He felt like a kid again, as tears stung his eyes. "I wasn't a good son to you, Matka Beth." The old word for mother came easily to his lips. "I need to apologize, and ask you to forgive me."

"Luke, we forgave you already, we did that a long time ago. You straightened yourself out, repaid the money you took. What more is there to forgive?" The older man assessed him shrewdly, as if he could discern Luke's soul.

Though that clear gaze didn't hold a trace of judgment, Luke stiffened and had to look away.

"Don't you think it's time you forgave yourself?" Stan asked.

Luke clenched his fists and bowed his head. Anger at himself for wrecking everything erupted like a volcano in his chest. "How can I? You helped me, you were good to me, and I betrayed your trust. I've ruined everything."

In the silence following his words, Luke stared at the pattern on the worn green carpet.

Stan reached over to the bookshelf and pulled out his worn old Bible, holding it in both hands as if touching it comforted him, even without opening it. "Why don't you tell us what's happened? Larry told us you were back in America. We figured you'd find us when you were ready."

Luke rubbed his face with both hands. "I discovered Anna didn't have Josh adopted, because he was ill as a baby. He won't get better, only worse. That's why I came back. I wanted to help her, and be a father to Josh. It felt like God's will, the right thing to do. Anna didn't want me around at first. Then she let me be part of Josh's life. He's a great kid. Brave, funny, with awesome faith."

Beth smiled encouragement. "I can see how proud you are of him. So what went wrong?"

Luke's lips tightened and he forced his stiff limbs to move him to the bookshelf. He picked up a small, misshapen clay dish, patchily glazed in green and brown. He'd made it for them, with love and care. But it was an ashtray, and the Kolinskys didn't smoke. His Mom was the one who smoked.

Even at ten, he'd got it wrong.

He carefully replaced the dish on the shelf, and shrugged. "I didn't tell her about my Mom, or being in foster care. I made my background sound better than it was. And I didn't tell her about the stealing or the drugs."

His voice cracked as guilt crashed down like a collapsing wall, crushing him beneath it.

Stan and Beth simply nodded, encouraging him to continue.

"Her father was a deputy. She believes strongly that crime must be punished. I knew I had to tell her, but how could I? I loved her back then. I love the woman she's become even more."

He fell silent, and a low groan escaped his lips as he thought of her. "How could I tell her I left my junkie Mom lying dead on the floor, and I stole from the only people who ever showed me kindness? And worse, stole to buy drugs?"

He heard Beth's intake of breath and Stan's heavy sigh, but neither of them spoke.

"She found out, anyway. Josh was on TV, and they filmed us too. Someone recognized me, told the town deputy, and he told her. He'd be a far better man for her than me."

"But does Anna love him?" Beth asked. "And does he love your son the way you do?"

Luke looked at her then, straight into her kind, earnest face. His breath caught in his throat and his heart twisted. "I'd started to hope Anna loved me again. And Josh…" His words trailed off and he shook his head, as love for his son exploded in his heart.

"No one except Anna could love Josh as much as I do. But I have no idea how to be a good father to him. You know apart from the couple of years I was with you I never had any sort of father. I failed with my Mom. I failed with Anna. I failed with you. What if I fail with him, too?"

He covered his face in his hands and dragged in a shaky breath, battling against a fresh crash of guilt that threatened to bury him for good.

Help me God, please. I don't know how to do this. Give me the strength to be the man I need to be.

Strong arms came around him, offering a father's comfort.

"Your mother took you away from us the first time. Your mistakes took you away the second time. But I'll always be your Tatko, your Dad."

Luke nodded, hearing the truth in Stan's words.

"And God is your Father too," Stan continued. "He loves you enough to call you His son. If you keep that in your heart, you won't fail in being a father. Or a husband, either. Beth and I forgive you. God forgives you."

He pushed Luke back, and looked him full in the face. "Now you only need forgive yourself. But there is one more person you need to talk to, before you can do that."

How did it all go wrong so fast?

Anna asked herself the question, over and over. The day that started badly with Luke looked set to end far worse.

Her heart thumped painfully as she sat in the examination room. Dr. Isaacs examined Josh, listening to his chest, asking him to breathe in, breathe out, over and over. But it was so much effort for Josh to breathe at all. She wanted to scream at the doctor. *Do something. Help him.* Her fingernails dug into her palms as she struggled to stay silent and let the doctor do her job.

The bright painted cartoon characters on the walls of the children's rooms and the colorful scrubs worn by the pediatric staff, supposedly cheerful and comforting, made her clench her teeth. Nothing but seeing Josh well again could soothe her.

Had there been signs she'd missed, things she should have noticed sooner?

Josh seemed fine when she said goodbye to him this morning, before Luke drove him to school. Tired after his busy weekend, but gleefully looking forward to his classmates' reaction to *Talent Trek*.

Then the phone call from the school, telling her he wasn't well. He'd insisted he was only tired, and his teacher was fussing about nothing. His breathing seemed normal. No cough or fever. Feeling wrung out, she'd let him overrule her instinct to take him straight to the doctor's office, and took him home instead.

That was where things went wrong.

Very, very wrong.

Josh hadn't improved. His temperature skyrocketed. His breathing became fast and labored. She recognized the signs, and now here they were, the ER at Orchard Bridge Memorial Hospital, in a room reeking of disinfectant and fear.

The triage nurse said nothing, but the stillness in her face as she'd written her readings on Josh's chart hadn't been reassuring. The fact the doctor saw them with hardly any wait was even less reassuring. Anna had learned enough in his previous admissions to know the numbers on his monitor weren't good. Without treatment, they wouldn't get any better.

Dr. Isaacs finished her exam and sat opposite Josh, pulling her chair near to his and leaning forward, her face serious and her hands clasped on her knees.

Anna sat beside him, his painful struggle for every breath sickening her with worry. Last time he'd been this ill, two winters ago, he'd nearly died. The doctors warned her if he developed pneumonia again he might not pull through another time.

She wished she could pray, but she couldn't.

Josh might die. And Luke wasn't here, because she sent him away.

CHAPTER TWENTY

ANNA'S TEETH CLAMPED HARD on her lower lip as she waited for Dr. Isaacs to speak. It wouldn't be anything she wanted to hear, she knew that.

"Josh, I think you have pneumonia," the doctor said. "A lung infection. You had it before, but you might not remember the doctors explaining it to you then. You know how when you have a cold you get a red runny nose?"

Josh nodded, but his brow creased. Anna saw the worry in his eyes. Probably, he remembered far too much of his last episode. He shouldn't have to suffer like this. It wasn't fair. What had he done to deserve it?

She took his hand and gently squeezed. His tense hand trembled in hers then clutched tight.

"Well this is the same, except it's in your lungs, inside your chest. Because your muscles aren't as strong as most peoples' are, you can't cough properly. Fluid builds up in your chest and makes it hard for you to breathe. Does that make sense?"

He nodded again. Talking was probably too much effort.

Anna struggled to stay silent. She wanted to shout at the doctor. *Don't waste time explaining. Can't you see how exhausted he is from the struggle?*

"We need to do an X-ray to be sure, but there are signs you have a lot of fluid in your chest. So I want to put you on a ventilator, a machine that breathes for you. We'll need to put a tube in your mouth so the machine works properly. Because that's uncomfortable to do when you're awake, I'd have to give you medicine to make you sleep, through a little needle in the back of your hand. It doesn't hurt any more than a lab draw. We'll keep you asleep until the strong antibiotics I'll prescribe make your lungs better, then we'll wake you up. Okay?"

Josh nodded, but when he turned his head toward her, Anna saw the fear shadowing his eyes. He was old enough and smart enough to know what all this meant. She squeezed his hand again.

"Dad?" She had to lean close to hear his thready voice.

"I texted him before we left home, and I'll text him again," she promised, closing her eyes for a moment as guilt tightened her throat.

She couldn't bear to see Josh's anxious face. He wanted his Dad. Luke would be here if she hadn't sent him away. But she'd had no way of knowing Josh would get so sick.

"He had to go to Eugene," she explained to the doctor. "But we can't wait for him, can we?"

The words barely made it past the huge angry knot of pain in her chest. It expanded to fill her entire being. Anger with Luke. Anger with herself. Anger with God for doing this to them.

She longed to let it go, surrender it all, hand it over to God, but she didn't know how. She'd been angry and fighting so long.

Dr. Isaacs shook her head. "We need to get things moving now." She patted Josh's shoulder. "Sorry, Josh. We can't wait for your Dad."

She turned to speak to the nurse, and the hospital team took over in a swirl of activity Anna had no control over. Everything felt sped up, jerky and disconnected, like a movie fast-forwarding.

Somehow, she held herself together. She had to, for Josh.

Inside, she disintegrated into a million tiny pieces, ready to explode.

At the billing clerk's painfully slow itemizing of what could happen if the county health plan didn't pay the hospital bills, she almost did. How could this woman not understand? She'd sell everything she owned if that was what it took to get Josh treatment.

Biting back the hasty words that rose to her mouth, she grabbed the forms from the clerk's hands, and signed without even reading them.

Josh was beyond brave, enduring lab draws, an X-ray, IV line insertion, and antibiotic administration. He tried to smile, but his hands and lips trembled. Propped up on the big hospital gurney, he shrank into himself, looking so fragile and small. His stiff thin shoulders rose and fell as he struggled to get air into his lungs.

She'd do anything, give anything, to save him from this.

If only she hadn't sent Luke away. Josh needed him here. And she did, too.

Luke shivered. A cold wind blew across the cemetery, and he'd left his jacket back in the truck at Stan and Beth's. They didn't seem to feel the chill. It must be only him, and that boulder of ice he carried in his gut.

He stood beside a grave, marked with a weather-worn timber cross bearing the name Mary Tanner, her birth and death dates just thirty-three years apart.

His mother.

Again, a tsunami of guilt and failure washed over him, threatening to lay him flat. Memories choked him. How could he forgive himself for leaving her, for not being able to stop her dying?

As if he knew Luke's thoughts, Stan spoke. "Yes, you need to forgive yourself. But first, you need to forgive her."

Luke opened his mouth to deny any need to forgive. Of course he wasn't angry with his mother. How could he be? She'd suffered so much.

Then he stopped. Words he'd said to Josh that first Sunday in Sweetapple Falls echoed in his mind.

You have every right to feel mad. It's staying mad that's the problem.

His heart pounded as the same hot rage he'd glimpsed and quickly suppressed that day rose in him again. That hurting angry kid inside him who wanted to scream "It's not fair! What about me?" and throw every tantrum he'd never been able to throw.

Who wanted to fling himself on the grave and pound his fists into the ground.

Who'd wanted to mean more to his Mom than the drugs did, after going to bed hungry so many nights and taking beating after beating while he tried to win some spark of love and approval from her.

That kid who never understood why he was forced to go back to her chaotic world when he was happy with Tatko and Matka.

He faced the dark abyss of his unconfessed anger. Not just with his Mom. With Stan and Beth, for letting him go. With God, for letting it happen. With himself.

He'd never given himself the right to be mad, so he'd *stayed* mad.

That anger and resentment he'd locked away, hidden in the dark where God's love couldn't reach it, had seeped into everything he'd done since. The real reason he felt guilty, couldn't believe God's love and forgiveness applied to him.

Now he had to let go, or he'd never be whole, never be able to live fully in the light. A heart holding so much bitterness could never taste the sweetness of life.

But how could he release something that had been part of him so long? Its roots had buried themselves deep into his heart, like ivy on an old brick wall. Rip off the ivy, and the roots would pull the crumbling bricks apart.

His fists clenched in frustration until his nails dug into his palms. He wanted to cry, but his burning eyes stayed dry. Tears would be too easy.

Father, help me. Shine Your light in my darkness. Show me how to let this anger go. Forgive me, and help me to forgive.

He looked at Matka and Tatko, watching him with anxious eyes.

They hadn't wanted to let him go. They'd had no choice but to give him back to Mom, when Social Services told them to. They were easy to forgive.

He dropped to his knees beside his mother's grave, and looked at those pitifully short dates. She hadn't chosen to love the drugs more than him. It was a sickness she couldn't control. She'd kept trying to clean up. Tried to get him back, refused to give him up for adoption.

She'd loved him as best as she could, in her broken confused way.

As for God, He gave us free will, then sent us Jesus when we misused it and messed up. That was love, more love than any of us deserved.

Luke sucked in a deep breath, allowed the anger to swell in him like a wave, and then surrendered it to God.

Without it, he caved in on himself, empty as a crumpled paper bag now the anger had gone. He breathed deep, staying with the emptiness, trusting God to fill him.

And God did.

Where the anger had hidden, forgiveness, peace, and love grew, blossoming like a garden full of flowers.

For the first time, Luke felt whole. For the first time, he felt truly his Father's son. Both God's son, and Tatko's. With fathers like that, he could be a good father to Josh.

And maybe, God willing, a good husband to Anna.

He knew what he had to do.

In the morning, he'd drive back to Sweetapple Falls, and the woman and son he loved. Even if Anna didn't want him, never forgave him, he'd be there for her and Josh. No matter how long it took, he'd prove he could be trusted and relied on.

With God's help, he'd do it.

Now the tears came, salt water cleansing his eyes and falling to the earth over his mother's grave. He let them fall, then kissed the fingers of one hand and laid it flat on the grass in front of the cross, saying the goodbye he'd never been able to say to her.

Heart full, he smiled up at Matka and Tatko, standing on the other side of the grave.

"Thank you."

Their loving smiles and the tears gleaming in their eyes showed they'd heard all the words he hadn't spoken.

He stood and linked arms with them, one each side. As they walked back to Tatko's car, anyone who saw them would think they were a family.

And that was what they were.

Anna paced beside the trolley transferring Josh to the PICU, another falsely cheerful room with falsely cheerful staff. The amount of equipment in the room they took him to scared her sick.

Pasting on a reassuring smile for him, she gulped air into her tight chest and forced her limbs not to quake.

After lifting Josh onto the bed, two nurses kindly but firmly pushed her aside as they attached him to monitors, explaining what they did as they went. He lay back against the pillows, eyes closed, mouth open under the oxygen mask, panting short gasping breaths.

His heart and breathing rates were worryingly high, his blood pressure and oxygen level scarily low. The nurses started preparing equipment on the cart behind him, drawing up medication and taping the vials to the syringes, attaching tubing to the ventilator.

Anna struggled to breathe herself, as fear tightened her throat.

He was in the right place.

They'd pulled him through last time. She had to keep reminding herself. She had to stay strong.

Dr. Isaacs hurried into the room, glanced at the preparations, and nodded to the nurses. "Josh, in a minute I'm going to give you the medicine that will make you fall asleep. Then we'll hook you up to the machine to help you breathe. We'll let you have a good long sleep. When you wake up, you'll still be attached to the machine, so you won't have to work so hard to breathe. Once you're breathing easily by yourself again, we'll take you off the machine. That might take a few days. Do you understand?"

Josh's eyes fluttered open, and he gave a barely perceptible nod.

Anna nodded, not trusting herself to speak. She bit her lip and clenched her fists to stop from trembling.

"Mom, do you want to stay here while we do this?" the doctor asked.

Somehow, Anna forced words past the massive lump in her throat. "Yes of course, if Josh wants me."

His nod was even weaker this time. Sweat beaded his forehead.

Please, hurry. Anna didn't say the words out loud. Fear wrenched her, fear Josh would die in front of them if they didn't get him onto breathing support fast.

She moved to his side and stood where the nurse told her, holding Josh's moist hand while the doctor inserted a syringe into his IV tubing.

"Here we go," Dr. Isaacs said. "Josh, you needn't do it out loud, but I want you to start counting to ten."

His hand twitched in Anna's with each number she counted for him. They got to five, then his hand went limp. "You'll be fine, kiddo. When you wake up, your dad will be here," she promised in a shaking voice, hoping that was true.

The team sprang into action and she stepped out the way, huddling in a chair against the wall as they lowered the back of the bed and started to work on Josh's motionless form. Stiff with tension, she covered her face with her hands, unable to watch.

Guide their hands, Lord. Guide their hands. Keep Josh alive.

The prayer played in her mind on an endless loop as her pulse pounded in her ears.

Then she heard the whir and hiss of the ventilator working, and someone touched her elbow. She opened her eyes. The doctor stood by her side. "It's safe to look now, Mom."

Josh lay flat in the bed, a tube strapped into his mouth, his eyes taped shut. He looked so lifeless beneath the white sheet. Her hand covered her mouth, holding back a sob.

Then she saw the monitors on the wall. That steady beep she heard was his heartbeat. Already, his pulse had slowed from the frantic rate the infection and his battle to breathe caused. Still way faster than it should be, but closer to normal.

Thank You. Thank You.

"All set. The ventilator is doing the work of breathing for him now." Dr. Isaacs smiled. "He's stable, though we won't know till later tonight if the infection is responding to the antibiotics or not."

"What if he doesn't respond?"

The smile faded from the doctor's face and her lips tightened. "He's on the strongest antibiotics we have. Let's pray he does respond." She squeezed Anna's elbow. "I'll be back later to reassess him."

The doctor left. The nurses bustled around a while longer, checking Josh's ventilator settings, showing Anna how to use the call bell, reassuring her that even if they weren't in the room, they'd be assessing the monitor readings and would come if needed.

Then she was left alone with Josh.

She pulled the chair to his bedside, and watched his chest rise and fall with the rhythmic shushing of the ventilator. His stillness alarmed her. At least he no longer struggled to breathe. The terrifying tension had left his muscles.

But he was still in danger. Josh might die, and she couldn't do a thing about it.

If only she'd recognized sooner that he was ill, taken him to the doctor straight away, maybe he wouldn't have got so sick.

Her life was full of "if onlys". If only Dad had forgiven her for getting pregnant with Josh, he might have supported her marrying Luke. If only she'd realized Luke would see her giving into to Dad as rejecting him, she could have handled it better, made sure he didn't leave them. If only she hadn't called Mom's cellphone, causing the crash that killed her parents. If only she hadn't told Luke to leave today.

If she hadn't, he'd be here at Josh's bedside too, his presence giving Josh the reassurance he needed. Maybe, if she hadn't made Luke go away, Josh wouldn't need to be here in the hospital at all.

She'd seen how disappointed Josh had been when she'd told him Luke had gone, the fear in his eyes that his Dad might not come back. That worry might have reduced his resistance to the infection.

Had she caused all this, by sending Luke away? The unanswerable question twisted a knife deep into her heart.

Every time she'd lost someone she loved, it had been her fault.

CHAPTER TWENTY-ONE

Anna bowed her head. She tried to pray for Josh, but couldn't find the words.

For the longest time, she'd felt God didn't listen to her.

Pastor Dan might talk about God's love and forgiveness, but she didn't feel it. Not one bit. Dad said God was the big Sheriff in the Sky, watching and waiting to punish any wrongdoing.

Well, she'd given Him plenty to punish. People at church even told her Josh's condition was a punishment for her sin. Dad implied that, too. He'd looked at her as if she was something dirty, stopped loving her as soon as he knew how she'd shamed him.

Wouldn't her heavenly Father feel the same? Josh would tell her God didn't work like that, but she wasn't so sure.

Anna lifted his frail limp hand from where it lay on the bed. The feel of his thin twisted fingers in hers ripped at her heart and wrenched her apart. It wasn't fair. Why should Josh suffer?

Doubled over in agony, she rested her head on the cool white sheet.

Why, God, why?

She asked the question over and over, not getting an answer. She wanted to bang her head against the wall, against the floor, anything to feel something besides this terrible rage at God and at herself.

Then other words seeped into her mind. Bible verses she'd learned in Sunday School when she was years younger than Josh, and won a bookmark with kittens on it for memorizing. Slowly, she focused, felt their calm and peace.

Our Father in heaven, hallowed be your name,
your kingdom come, your will be done,
on earth as it is in heaven.
Give us today our daily bread.
And forgive us our debts,
as we also have forgiven our debtors.
And lead us not into temptation,
but deliver us from the evil one.
For yours is the kingdom, and the power, and the glory, for ever.
Amen.

She'd heard it so many times before, but hadn't understood.

God had forgiven her all along. He was the only Father whose approval mattered now.

But she'd never feel forgiven, by God or anyone else, until she forgave. Starting with forgiving God. He wasn't punishing her for her mistakes, had never punished her. She'd been the one to punish herself, and Luke too.

She'd blamed Luke for leaving her when she'd agreed to Josh's adoption, held on to her oh-so-righteous anger and lack of trust like a shield. Today, she'd judged him exactly the same way Dad had judged her. She'd believed Luke lied because he didn't love her or trust her enough to tell the truth.

No. He'd lied because he knew she wouldn't forgive him for shattering her fairy-tale demands for the man she'd fall in love with. The flawless hero in glittering silver armor on a snow-white horse. An impossible ideal no real man could live up to.

I forgive him for lying to me. I forgive him for not telling me about his past. Forgive me, God, please forgive me. And help me to forgive myself.

Huge shuddering sobs wracked her body, and she stuffed her hands into her mouth to muffle them. Tears flooded down her face. The tears she'd never cried when Luke went away, or when Josh was diagnosed. When Dad stopped loving her, or when her parents died.

She'd never grieved. She'd just gotten angry, and stayed angry. But her anger hurt her far more than anyone else.

Surrendering to the torrent of emotion flooding her, she sobbed out her pain and rage and loss. And she felt God there with her, really truly there with her. A loving presence, telling her she was forgiven, it was safe to love, safe to trust.

It took Luke coming back into her life to show her how trapped in her anger and fear she'd been. She'd believed she couldn't trust Luke, because it was safer not to trust. She'd believed she'd lose everyone she loved sooner or later, so it was safer not to love. She'd believed that she couldn't be forgiven, so she couldn't forgive anyone else.

Somehow, she'd thought staying angry with Luke would get her father's love back. But all she'd done was close herself off to love.

Luke's love. And God's.

At last the storm passed, and she raised her head, reaching for tissues to mop her face.

Josh lay still and motionless, appearing unchanged. But the monitors told another story. His heart rate had lowered. His temperature had dropped. His oxygen level had improved. Signs the treatment was starting to work.

Tears sprang to her eyes again, tears of joy this time. Gratitude blossomed in her like a rose.

Thank You, Lord. Thank You. Thank You for healing Josh, and thank You for healing me.

But now she'd forgiven Luke, could he forgive her? She'd done her best to hurt him and drive him away.

What if she'd succeeded?

Home from the cemetery, Luke thanked God for his foster parents' love.

Matka and Tatko gladly welcomed him to stay the night. They cooked a simple meal together, in the small kitchen filled with love and laughter. When they sat to eat, Tatko's heartfelt prayer of thanksgiving warmed his heart as surely as Matka's good cooking.

Long after they'd finished eating, they sat around the table, sharing stories of House the World, of Anna and Josh, of Stan and Beth's life since he'd gone away. It felt good to be home.

And tomorrow, home to Sweetapple Falls, to the life-long job of being Josh's dad and proving to Anna she could trust him again.

"Time for bed, I think, son," Stan said eventually. "An early night means an early start in the morning. You'll be back with your Anna and Josh sooner."

Luke grimaced. "Anna probably won't want to see me. But I have to be there if she needs me. I'll get my things from the truck."

As he carried his overnight bag and jacket into the house, his cellphone beeped. Dropping his bag, he pulled the phone from his jacket pocket. Two messages, both from Anna.

Apprehension skittered along his nerves. She wouldn't text unless it was serious.

He read the messages. Read them again, praying he'd misunderstood.

He hadn't.

Dread slammed his chest, sledgehammer hard. Stunned and disbelieving, he turned to his foster parents. "I'm sorry. I have to go right now. It's Josh. He's in the hospital. Anna sent the first message hours ago, and I didn't see it."

He hugged them quickly, ran to his truck, and drove into the night, their promises to pray for Josh echoing in his ears.

Thankfully, the traffic wasn't heavy, though he thumped the steering wheel in frustration at every red light.

Please, Lord, be with Anna and Josh. Keep him safe. Let me get there in time.

At last he reached the highway and could push the old truck to its top speed. Fear wrapped cold hands around his throat, strangling him. All he could do was pray harder. At last, heart racing, he parked outside the hospital and rushed to the entrance.

"PICU?" he asked the tired woman at Reception.

"Through those doors and up the stairs, but they're closed to visitors now."

Waving thanks, he was at the doors before she finished. He took the stairs two at a time, then slammed his hand against the PICU door.

It didn't budge.

Too late, he saw the sign and the security lock. Forcing himself to drag in a deep breath and calm down, he looked for the intercom, and jammed his finger against the button.

"Luke Tanner," he said, the second someone answered. "Josh Harrison's father."

"You can come in. First room on the left." The door buzzed and clicked as it unlocked.

Breathing a silent prayer, Luke pushed the door open and went to the room.

Josh lay motionless as a rag doll on the hospital bed, a tube in his mouth and others in his arms, hooked up to machines that beeped and whirred. Anna huddled beside him.

Luke's heart clenched at the sight of his son, so still and so vulnerable. The numbers flashing on the monitors meant nothing to him. He had no way of knowing if Josh was okay or not. Nothing he could do would help his son. Feeling so powerless wrung him dry.

But there was one thing he could still do.

Pray.

Father, keep him safe. Bring him back to us, please.

Anna sat slumped in a chair next to Josh, her head on his bed, hair falling across her face. Her closed eyes were red-rimmed and puffy, her skin almost as white as the sheet she lay on. One hand lay over Josh's, the other hung by her side. She looked exhausted.

And beautiful. So beautiful.

Luke drank her in. He could never get enough of her.

She opened her eyes, blinked blearily, then pushed herself upright. A joyous smile he hadn't expected lit her face.

Double relief flooded Luke. Anna wouldn't smile like that if Josh was still in danger.

And she seemed happy to see him.

He spread his arms wide, and she ran right into them.

As Luke's strong arms closed around her, Anna knew she'd come home at last. Home to the man God always intended for her, now she'd grown up enough to love him right.

He'd come back. Her whole being sang with thanksgiving as she rested her head against his broad chest and his heartbeat thundered in her ear. He lowered his head till his cheek rested on her hair. She felt so safe, so willing to trust him.

Though she still didn't know what his return meant for her.

His warm comforting embrace didn't mean he'd forgiven her for doubting him, and for sending him away.

She pulled back a little and looked up into his face. His steady gaze on her held a love that took her breath away, though his eyes and forehead creased in concern.

Joy swelled her heart, and she smiled. God had given her so much more than she deserved.

"Josh?" he asked, keeping his hands firm and comforting on her shoulders.

Tears sprang to her eyes, and Luke's grip tightened. A look of painful anxiety crossed his face, making her heart quiver.

She rushed to reassure him. "No, Josh is doing okay now. These are happy tears." Her shoulders slumped. "It was scary for a while. He got so tired. I thought he might stop breathing." Remembered fear chilled her and she fell silent, recalling Josh's struggle to get air into his lungs, the terror in his eyes, the way his hand had clutched hers.

Luke looked down for a second, then his dark eyes rose to meet hers, warm with sincerity.

"I'm sorry I wasn't here for you both. I hope Josh never gets so ill again, but if he does, you won't need to go through it alone. I'll be with you."

She nodded, willing at last to believe him, all doubt gone. "I know that, Luke."

So much warm gladness lit his eyes she almost melted.

A knock at the door interrupted them, and Dr. Isaacs stepped into the room. She stared at Josh's still form, at his chart, at the monitors, and nodded, with a satisfied smile. "His numbers are a lot better. He seems to be responding well to the antibiotics."

She looked at Luke.

"This is Luke Tanner, Josh's father," Anna said, pride ringing in her voice.

She felt it. His past didn't matter anymore. All that counted was who he'd become. She hoped he'd think the same about her.

But for now, Josh was their main priority.

Dr. Isaacs shook Luke's hand in her no-nonsense manner. "Does he know you're here?"

Luke shook his head.

"Well, come over here and talk to him," she said. "He's sedated, in a kind of sleep, but in my experience patients still have some awareness of what's around them, hearing most of all. Just talk to him like you normally would. I'd like to see if he responds."

Luke rushed to Josh's bedside and lifted the boy's limp hand. "Hi Josh, it's me, Dad. I'm sorry I wasn't here when you got sick."

He looked up, a plea for reassurance he was doing it right in his eyes. Anna knew how disconcerting and worrying Josh's lack of response felt.

The doctor nodded, and Luke spoke again.

"I needed to visit my foster parents. They want to come to Sweetapple Falls and meet you when you're well again. Last time they saw you, you were a tiny baby. But guess what? They know someone in their church who has a spare video camera to give away. They're going to bring it with them when they visit."

Anna stayed silent, holding her breath, praying Josh would give whatever sign the doctor wanted to see.

Dr. Isaacs nodded. "His heart rate increased when you spoke to him. Good. I'll listen to his chest now."

She pulled out her stethoscope, and bent over Josh's still form. When she straightened, her smile was all the reassurance Anna needed.

"For tonight, we'll keep him sedated and let the machine do all the work, to give him a rest. But there's a chance he might be able to start breathing for himself tomorrow. It will be a long haul, but I think he's turned the corner."

She made a few notes on Josh's chart, and bustled out of the room.

Anna pressed both hands to her chest. Relief and elation could float her away like a helium balloon.

Thank You, Lord. Thank You.

Luke lifted tear-bright eyes to her and beamed. He turned back to the still figure on the bed. "Josh, did you hear what the doctor said? You're getting better."

Anna watched the monitor as Luke spoke. She saw it too, the small but definite rise in the heart rate.

"He heard you," she said. "He heard you." She buried her face in her hands and sobbed.

Luke's arms came around her again, and he held her while she wept, unashamed of her weakness.

She lifted her face to his. "He's going to make it, isn't he? He's really going to pull through this."

He nodded, and lifted a gentle hand to brush the tears from her cheeks. His cheeks were just as wet. Laughing, she raised both her hands to wipe his face, his stubble rough beneath her palms.

"We're a pair," she said, voice unsteady.

Luke's eyes grew serious. "I hope so, Anna. I want us to be. But can you forgive me for letting you down, and not telling you the truth?"

She held his face in her hands and gazed into his eyes. She saw forever reflected there, the love she'd always hoped for and never dared believe in.

God whispered one word to her. *Believe.*

Joy expanded her heart so much it hurt. A good pain. The kind she wanted to feel for the rest of her life. She blinked back fresh tears at the wonder of it all.

"Of course I forgive you. I'm the one who doesn't deserve your forgiveness. I expected so much of you. I stayed angry so long, so focused on the past I couldn't see the man you'd become." She dragged in a shaky breath. "I love you, Luke Tanner."

The delight in his gaze gave her all the answer she needed. His lips lowered to hers, stopping her words and showing her just how real his forgiveness and love was.

Just when she'd thought she'd lost it all, she'd been blessed with everything she'd most longed for.

He lifted his head, and his strong hands cupped her face. "And I love you." Emotion roughened his voice as he looked into her eyes. "I thought I'd lost my chance to have a family. And then, when I least expected it, God gave me a second chance with you. Will you let me make us a real family?"

Her laugh was shaky as her heart overflowed. "I don't deserve you." She touched his strong lips with trembling fingertips, feeling as well as seeing them quirk in a smile.

"And I don't deserve you either. None of us deserve love, and yet we're loved anyway. That's the blessing of grace. We'll just need to keep on asking God's help to be worthy of each other. Marry me, Anna."

She smiled, nodded, and lifted her head for his kiss.

His lips on hers were a promise of a shared future with no more secrets to divide them.

They'd both been given a second chance.

EPILOGUE

Luke's heart pounded with mingled joy and nerves as he stood at the front of the church waiting for Anna.

Seemed as if almost everyone in Sweetapple Falls had crowded in for the ceremony. His past was now public knowledge, but few people showed they judge him for it.

Even Tabby Whytecliff was here, though maybe more because she didn't want to miss out than because she approved of him.

Dan, standing in front of him ready to conduct the service, gave an encouraging smile.

Josh looked up from fiddling with his video camera to grin. He'd been planning his best man's speech for weeks, and working out how to film the ceremony. Thankfully, setting up his TV channel and the wedding plans had eased his disappointment at missing the *Talent Trek* tour.

Luke eyed him anxiously, checking his breathing rate. He'd made a faster recovery that his doctors expected from pneumonia, but even three months later they needed to make sure he didn't overdo things. His dark formal suit swamped his too-thin arms and legs, but he looked fine.

The sound of a car door outside and a low murmur from the congregation set Luke's heart racing. Everyone swiveled to watch the doorway.

Lamorna's high sweet voice rose in the simple tune and meaningful words of Anna's chosen wedding song, *Household of Faith*. The pure haunting tones echoed through the church. When Josh suggested asking Lamorna to sing, some folk said they were taking forgiveness too far.

But Luke had learned, it wasn't possible to do that. True forgiveness has no limits.

He craned his neck, longing for a glimpse of Anna. The woman he intended to love and cherish for the rest of his life. She stepped through the tall wooden doors, leaning on Stan's arm, and her beauty caught the breath in his throat.

Her floor length white dress looked perfect on her, proclaiming their new beginning, the start of a brand new life for all of them. The lilacs she'd hoped to carry were finished now, so instead she held a small bunch of creamy roses from her garden, roses her great-grandmother planted and her grandmother and mother had tended. Her eyes met his and her lips trembled in a shy smile.

His grin felt so wide it could crack his face. He couldn't take his gaze away from her.

Her walk down the aisle took forever, but at last she was beside him.

The song ended. In the silence all he could hear was his own pulse, thundering in his ears. Stan smiled as he placed Anna's hand on Luke's outstretched arm, then stepped back to sit with Beth in the front row.

Anna's hand quivered, and he covered it with his, though emotion shook his just as much. He searched her face, wanting to make sure she had no doubts.

Her fingers tightened. Her smile and nod and the look of joyous certainty in her eyes swept away any lingering anxiety that she might have changed her mind. He still couldn't quite believe he'd been blessed so abundantly.

Maggie moved to stand on Anna's other side, resplendent in purple, eyes alight with mischief. Luke saw why. Pattie Pork Pie trotted proudly beside her on a leash, wearing a tutu in matching purple.

Luke laughed and shook his head.

Anna smiled and whispered, "Josh's idea."

His son's grin and raised hand ready for a high five told him all he needed to know.

He should have guessed his unconventional family would have a surprise for him. He high fived Josh, then turned to Dan and nodded. They were ready.

As Dan began the words of the wedding service that would make them husband and wife, Luke gave silent thanks.

Their mistakes had taken them far from each other. They'd had lessons to learn about trust, forgiveness, and second chances. But at last, with God's perfect timing, he, Anna and Josh were becoming the forever family he knew God intended them to be all along.

Love won. With God, love always won.

THE END

THANK YOU FOR READING…

I hope you enjoyed reading His Father's Son! Thank you for spending this time with my story. I pray that you feel God's love, mercy, and grace richly blessing your life!

This story is close to my heart, as it was my first completed Christian romance! I learned so much writing it, and the process brought me much closer to God. It's been through a lot of revisions and edits since then! I still get teary for the characters and all they go through and need to learn before they can commit to their lifetime of love together, every time I read it. Thankfully, God's grace and forgiveness are real, and His love does always win!

If you liked this story, you'll probably also enjoy my other books. There's the *Love in Store* series set mainly in London; *The Macleans* series, set mostly in Edinburgh; *Huckleberry Lake*, set in Idaho; and many other books to come.
Most of my stories aren't quite as heart-wringing than this one, but all include love, faith, characters overcoming real issues, and always, always ALWAYS, a happy ever after!
You can see all my currently released boioks on my website books page: www.FaithHopeandHeartwarming.com

Also, if you enjoyed this book, please consider telling other readers and posting a short review on Amazon, Goodreads, or anywhere else readers discuss books. Recommendations from happy readers are so very appreciated by authors, and it helps readers find books they like. Your opinion counts!

Blessings, and happy reading!

Autumn♥

BIBLE VERSES

<u>Chapter 1</u>
Greater love has no one than this: to lay down one's life for one's
friends.
John 15:13 NIV

<u>Chapter 2</u>
I can do all things through Christ who strengthens me
Philippians 4:13 NKJV

<u>Chapter 8</u>
"In your anger do not sin": Do not let the sun go down while you are
still angry
Ephesians 4:26 NIV

<u>Chapter 13</u>
There is no fear in love. But perfect love drives out fear, because fear
has to do with punishment. The one who fears is not made perfect in
love.
1 John 4:18 NIV

<u>Chapter 19</u>
Love the Lord your God with all your heart and with all your soul
and with all your mind and with all your strength.' The second is this:
'Love your neighbor as yourself.' There is no commandment greater
than these."
Mark 12:30-31 NIV

For I know the plans I have for you," declares the Lord, "plans to
prosper you and not to harm you, plans to give you hope and a
future.
Jeremiah 29:11 NIV

<u>Chapter 20</u>
For God so loved the world that he gave his one and only Son, that
whoever believes in him shall not perish but have eternal life.
John 3:16 NIV

Chapter 21
"This, then, is how you should pray:
'Our Father in heaven,
hallowed be your name,
your kingdom come,
your will be done,
   on earth as it is in heaven.
Give us today our daily bread.
And forgive us our debts,
   as we also have forgiven our debtors.
And lead us not into temptation,
   but deliver us from the evil one.'
Matthew 6:9-13 NIV□

Stay up to date with my new releases as well as special subscriber-only freebies and special offers, by signing up for my mailing list. Sign-up links can be found at my website www.autumnmacarthur.com or by scanning the QR code.